SINCE YOU ASK

a novel by

Louise Wareham

AKASHIC BOOKS
New York

Published by Akashic Books
©2004 Louise Wareham
Layout by Sohrab Habibion

ISBN: 1-888451-63-7
Library of Congress Control Number: 2003116589
All rights reserved
First printing
Printed in Canada

Akashic Books
PO Box 1456
New York, NY 10009
Akashic7@aol.com
www.akashicbooks.com

To my family

Acknowledgments

Thank you Isabel Huggan, my mentor. Thank you Kaylie Jones and the James Jones Literary Society, Kim Witherspoon and Alexis Hurley, Charles Baxter, and Bill Black.

Thanks to Daniel and Jamie Gerard, Kimberly Malloy, and Jake Boone.

Thanks to Richard Hire, Lana Santorelli, Rose Cook, and my own personal old-timers: Eric, Larry, John Romeo, Kevin, Eileen, and Stacey.

Thank you Carter Cooper, 1965–1988, and Evan, always missed.

Most of all, and every day, thank you Margaret, my mother, and Margaret Patterson, unbelievable, irrepressible, most excellent of friends.

PART I

LAST MAY MY whole family drove out to JFK Airport to meet Raymond. He had been gone for six years, and Dad was carrying his camera as if Ray were some kind of movie star. Usually, I was nervous around Ray, but I wasn't that day. Partly because I didn't live at home anymore and partly because Ray didn't bother me anymore.

'Give your brother a kiss,' my mother said, prodding me in the back.

'Put your arm around her,' Dad said, pointing his camera at us. Then Eric stood between us and Dad took pictures of that, too.

In the car, we passed rows and rows of housing projects, all square and brown and the same. I would have to kill myself if I lived in a place like that. I pointed this out, but no one said anything.

Raymond lit a cigarette when he stepped out of the car. Couldn't you wait, I wanted to say. He had a few drags, then flicked it to the gutter. We went to Sardi's. It was loud and crowded, and Dad ordered wine and pasta with clams. He gave a toast to Raymond, 'our prodigal son.' I looked at Eric, but he didn't seem to notice. Raymond set his glass on the table and tapped his fingers. Then he went to the bathroom.

Dr. Keats, my psychiatrist here, says I am too 'fragmented.' I am overwhelmed, he says. My mind is overwhelmed and for this reason it has begun to crack, or 'break.' He doesn't say this in a mean way, but in a way I will understand. I do understand, too. I am glad he says this because it is true. It is frightening and it is true.

After dinner, Dad dropped me off at 46th and Ninth. I had a sublet there: one room with a platform bed and a table overlooking the airshaft. The building was full of dance studios. I could hear African drums sometimes, or the footsteps of ballet classes. My place belonged to a ballet dancer; she had gone to Europe for a year. As soon as I got inside, I wanted to go out again. No one was around, though. Sylvia was at Yale, and Henry was in the Hamptons. I turned the television on, then off. I sat on my bed and looked through my phone book and finally, I called Beck.

We had met on the street, six years ago. Even then, when he was eighteen, he was the best-looking boy I had ever seen. He was grown like a man and as serious, leaning against a car with his arms on his chest, staring at me.

Now he was a corrections officer at the Tombs. He came over and sat on my bed, lighting matches with one hand. 'Oh, Betsy,' he said. 'Betsy, Betsy.'

'What?' I asked.

'You're all grown up. You've got this apartment and all your books.' He dropped his hand to my knee. 'Can I?'

Then he took off my clothes, and his. He ran his hand between my legs, and his tongue. Guys liked that, he said; I liked it, too. Only then he got rough, the way he always did.

Fairley has a swimming pool and a tennis court, but they're kind of depressing. First of all, who wants to play tennis in a mental institution? Second, the pool is like an old person's pool: all dark and clammy. If I kill myself here, I am going to walk into the pool with rocks in my pockets. Even though this is a mental hospital, we don't have locked wards. It is the kind of place where you could walk with rocks into the pool and no one would notice.

Beck stayed until six a.m. Then he left a note by my bed: *Beck + Betsy.* This made me feel bad—mostly because it wasn't true, and also because I shouldn't have called him up that way.

'What way?' Dr. Keats asks.

'The day Raymond came home.'

'You feel that you used him?'

'I don't know about that. I do call him at pretty weird times. I met him just before Raymond went away.'

Keats's eyes lighten. 'You mean, before he left six years ago?'

I would like to be an interesting patient to him.

'Yes.'

⚜

I liked the morning hour between seven and eight. It was quiet, subdued. I held onto Beck's scrap of paper and finally, I got up. I put on a white shirt and a cotton skirt and I walked to work the way I always did, across 42nd Street to the East River. I stopped at the river, and the sunlight was gleaming off the water. I went up to World Sight and sat at my desk—pretending to read, but not reading, just thinking.

Ray had been back in the city for about eighteen hours when Dad brought him by for lunch. I went down to the cool glass lobby, light shimmering off the white marble. My father was wearing one of his expensive suits and smelled of citrus, of this English aftershave made for noblemen in 1861, that's what the bottle said. Ray smelled of cigarettes and cherry cough drops. We still hadn't said more than ten words to each other. Maybe he was embarrassed, having being in prison for so long.

'Show him around,' Dad said. 'Introduce him to some people,' as if this would be exciting for me. He went up to 6 to visit Wayne, and I took Ray to 3, down the long white corridors to the lab where I worked.

Ray's white wool sweater was grubby under Dad's blazer. 'So this it?' he asked. 'The famous Institute?'

'I guess.'

I showed him my workstation, a section of a long black counter. A lab technician, Diane, was there, and I introduced them.

'Pretty girl,' Ray said.

I tipped my coffee into the sink.

'You see much of Wayne?' he asked.

Wayne was a director at the Institute. He had grown up with my parents in London, and we had known him always, Ray and Eric and I, since we were born.

'Sure I do.'

'Really?'

'I work for him.'

Dad took Wayne and Ray and me to lunch, up a flight of cobblestone steps to *Le Balcon,* across from the UN. From our table, we could see the river, shadowy bluish gray. Dad ordered for everyone: wine and oysters and sea bass. A week ago, my father had said Ray was going straight from the airport to rehab. Now that he was home, no one mentioned rehab at all.

↝

We were born in Antigua: Raymond and Eric and I. Dad's first job was for the English government, working on Antigua's independence. Each night, I waited on the porch for him to come home, up the dusty hill in his creased linen shirt and his tan pants. He picked me up off the porch, salt coming off the ocean and metal slapping on the mast of our boat—*Stewball,* she was called, after Dad's favorite song:

> *Old Stewball was a racehorse and I wish he were mine,*
> *he never drank water, he always drank wine.*

We sailed her all around the island, to Barbuda and St. Kitts. We moored in the pale blue bays and swam to shore in the morning. We climbed the hillsides, through the loblolly and lantana where the jaquina smelled like honeysuckle.

Now Dad is a corporate lawyer for Thomas Tripp Stanton Geary & Scott. His office is on 50th Street and Sixth Avenue, in a row of skyscrapers. On his wall are all these photographs of my mother and Raymond and Eric and me. In most of them, we're on

Stewball, tanned and half-naked. 'What a good-looking family,' people always say, when they see these photos.

The best thing to be at Fairley is an alcoholic. They have affairs and steal all the Oreos and play guitar on the Dobson House porch. Once I went to Bishop House, where the depressives are, and everyone was sitting on the blue couch, watching television. Their faces were stiff from their medications. Alcoholics aren't supposed to be given medication—though they usually are.

I have been in Fairley for two months now. In Session, Dad says he wants me out of here as soon as possible. Keats says this is only the beginning of my 'recovery,' that I should stay at Fairley as long as my insurance will allow, then go to a good 'aftercare facility.' Dad doesn't want this. Dad doesn't want me here at all. He says I just like the attention.

We have lunch in Dining Hall, herbed salmon and green beans, and I get tremors in my hands from medication and also nervousness, I guess. My parents' faces turn a strange shade of gray, as if they are living through a catastrophe. I feel bad for them, especially for the Wayne part.

'Why Wayne?' Dr. Keats asks me later.

'He tried to help.'

'And where is he now?'

'In Belgium.'

'And where are you?'

Most of the time, my parents are very dazzling. They walk around like movie stars, kissing each other and wearing suede jackets. My mother is 5'7" and wears 3" heels. Sometimes, when she has just taken a bath, for example, it is a surprise to find that we are the same height. Her hair is the color of white honey, her eyes wide and pale blue. Eric inherited both of these features. People say this is a shame, since I am the girl, but I don't mind. Ray and I have my Dad's coloring, which is darker.

The truth is, Dad is right. I do like the attention. I like it when everyone sits around and discusses me. I like the plans and deliberations. I like being in the hospital, in general.

At first, I figured I would see Ray at family functions—on holidays and birthdays—and that would be it. Then, he called me the day after *Le Balcon*. It was ten-thirty at night, and I was watching some movie awards.

'What is it?' I asked.

'Nothing.'

He must have called for some reason, though he never got to it. He asked what I was doing and I told him. Then he asked me who my favorite actor was and I said Daniel Day-Lewis and then he hung up.

Two days later, he called me from his bedroom. Dad had been taking him around, he said, introducing him to his friends. 'He wants me to join his club.'

'Are you going to?'

'It's a pretty nice club. On 68th Street. They have a pool and masseuse.'

'So join.'

'I don't know. You have to talk to everyone all the time—the doorman and the pros and the members.'

I didn't know what to say to him, so I didn't say much, really.

Then it was Saturday morning and my doorbell rang, and I heard his voice through the intercom. It was like my lungs stopped. I had to wait a minute before I could speak, and finally, I told him I would come down.

He was leaning against the wall by the buzzers, in a beat-up corduroy jacket, a sort of dark yellow.

'What are you doing?' I asked.

'Just walking around.'

I remembered what my mother had said, just before Ray came home. She had said it would be hard for Ray, that six years was a long time to be away and he wouldn't know anyone now.

He would be lonely and we should be nice to him.

'You look pretty,' he said, and I did a small double-take on him then; it was the first time he had said that, ever.

We walked over to Sheep's Meadow in Central Park. The grass was long and green. Some school kids were playing guitar, and Ray didn't look like anyone there, with his paleness and his thinness and his black shirt buttoned at the wrists.

'So what do you do for fun?' he asked.

'Read. Go to the movies, parties.'

'You know of any parties now?'

'No.'

'You have any friends at the Institute?'

'Wayne.'

'You should stay away from Wayne.'

'Why should I?'

Raymond leaned back against an elm tree. 'You just should.'

I thought it was pretty funny that Raymond would tell me to stay away from anyone.

We went to Denzi's, off Madison Avenue on 63rd Street. Our table was small and round and white marble, just on the sidewalk. Raymond smoked and drank beer and pushed back his lanky hair. He leaned in and took a cigarette from my shirt pocket. Then he told me about prison and how he never should have been in there, how they made an example of him because our family was white and had money. The truth was that my father found the best lawyers in three countries to get Raymond out of jail. Truth was he had been sentenced to ten years and only served ten months.

'How's it going?' Wayne asked me on Monday at work, looking up from his desk.

'Okay.' I sat on his bright cranberry-colored couch, the coffee table littered with Evian bottles and newspapers.

'What's it like having Ray back?'

'It's not bad.'

Wayne was like a real brother, like a brother is supposed to be. He talked to me.

'We're getting along.'

'Your mother says he's doing well.'

'Maybe he is.'

I liked the Institute, working nine to five, walking to work all the way east across 42nd Street. I liked the clean white hallways and the smell of the river, the lattice windows with thick glass panes. Sometimes, Wayne opened his windows and we smoked a cigarette together. At the end of May, we took his car uptown for my mother's birthday. Wayne had an old navy blue BMW with wind-down windows and a stick shift. He opened up his sunroof on the FDR Drive, going uptown beside the river. The light shone on the silver streaks in his otherwise brown hair. He got better looking as he aged, my mother said. His face was lean, his nose aquiline. He was too skinny, but it suited him, somehow, would have made him winsome if he had been a woman.

'What did you get your mother?' he asked me.

'A scarf.'

'That's nice.'

He smoked like someone who had just started to smoke, squinting his eyes.

'What did you get?' I asked.

'I forgot, actually. You don't think she'll mind?'

'No.'

Wayne and my parents had grown up in London. After his first wife died, he came sometimes to visit us in Antigua. Once, when I was twelve, I saw him with my mother up on Shirley Heights, in the bar in the ruins of an old fort. It was Christmas and the walls were strung with tiny colored lights. The wind smelled of salt and Wayne and my mother were dancing. He had a slight stoop, as if from shyness, though he wasn't shy. He was more self-deprecating than shy. His hand was on the small of my mother's back. She had a drink in her hand and was leaning into him. Then he whispered something to her, and they turned and walked off down the hill.

* * *

My parents live in a townhouse on 64th Street between Lexington and Park, three stories high with a brown stoop and a garden out back. Wayne prodded me in the back when the door opened. It was my mother, of course, in a cream white suit and high-heeled sandals, toenail polish like mother-of-pearl. Wayne cupped her head in his hand.

'Only God, my dear, could love you for yourself alone, and not your yellow hair,' he said, not so unusually.

I could almost feel her smooth soft hair in his hand. I could almost hear his breath. It annoyed me, the way he touched her all the time, like she was some precious object. I gave her the box with the scarf in it and went back into the house, past the staircase on the left and the open dining room on the right, down a step into the living room. It was bright. The garden doors were open, late sun on the slate slabs. Ray was on the silk blue couch, a pale blue like the tropical blue of a bird. Eric was in a chair, one leg crossed over the other.

'Hey,' he said.

'Hey.'

He had just been awarded a fellowship at Yale Drama School. We weren't supposed to talk about it, because it might make Raymond feel bad.

Ray stood up. 'You want a drink, Eric?'

'No.'

'Smoke?'

'No.'

He laughed. 'You don't do much, do you?'

I felt bad for him, then, trying to insult Eric. Maybe that's why I went out with him later. Eric went up to his room. Wayne and my parents went to Dad's club and Dad gave Ray a $100 bill. 'Take Betsy out,' he said. 'Go and hear some jazz.'

We didn't go to hear jazz, but to Trader Vics at the Plaza Hotel. The walls were dark wood like the cabin of a ship, the plants stiff and green and waxy. Our table had a candle in a globe. Ray ordered beer and a piña colada for me. The place was full of girls in headbands and pearls, and Raymond didn't fit in at all, with his slick hair and black jeans and black cotton shirt. I saw two people from high school: Billy Kraze, who was at Wharton, and Ellen Drake, who slashed her wrist junior year.

'So how's your boyfriend?' Ray asked.

'I don't have a boyfriend.'

'I thought he went to reform school.'

'Oh, Beck. He's not my boyfriend.'

'You see him, though?' he asked.

'Sometimes.'

He tipped his beer glass back and forth. His fingernails were bitten down, the edges soft and papery.

'You still want to be a doctor?' he asked.

'Yes.'

"What are you going to do about med school?'

'I deferred. Didn't you know that?'

I had wanted to be a doctor since I was ten, since I fell down the cliff at Pigeon Point and broke my leg. I was in the hospital for two weeks, a Catholic hospital where the Sisters hung needlepoint above the bed: Jesus with his yellow hair, quotes from the prayer book decorated with flowers and little crosses.

> *Oh Jesus, bless my father, my mother, my brothers.*
> (Page 26, PRAYER FOR OTHERS)

> *Oh Jesus, may I lead a good life; may I die a happy death.*
> (Page 26, PRAYER FOR YOURSELF)

I copied out my own one day, using the 36-pastel-crayon set my father had bought me.

> *Oh my God, I am sorry and beg pardon for all my sins and detest them above all things, because they deserve your dreadful punishments.*
> (Page 9, ACT OF CONTRITION)

Sister Megan was upset at this. 'What have you done, Betsy,' she asked, 'that you are so sorry about?'

I didn't tell her.

'So what kind of doctor do you want to be?' Raymond asked.

'I don't know.'

'You could be anything, anything you wanted.'

꙳

'So why did you start spending time with Raymond,' Dr. Keats asks, 'considering how you felt about him?'

The sun slips between his wooden shutters. My legs are glossy with lotion. I swing my foot against the floor in its flat brown sandal.

'Sylvia was at Yale. Henry was in the Hamptons. And he was *different*. He was nice. Also, you know, my parents said he was *"so far behind me,"* that I was so *"beyond him."*'

'And you believed that?'

'I guess I did.'

Fairley has a small square library in the doctors' office, an empty desk with a stack of Fairley postcards of Main House in the 1950s. There are two reading chairs with cracked green leather. I copy down a poem from John Berryman and give it to Dr. Keats.

> *I'm too alone. I see no end. If we could all*
> *run, even that would be better. I am hungry.*
> *The sun is not hot.*
> *It's not a good position I am in.*
> *If I had to do the whole thing over again*
> *I wouldn't.*

꙳

One thing you have to understand is that Raymond had always been on drugs. When I was twelve, my parents sat me down and told me that Raymond was a junkie and could die at any time. Also, I did drugs myself, in high school mostly, with my friend Sylvia Goldfarb Davis. We did cocaine in our school basement and the theater and the bathrooms. We did it at her house, drinking soda and listening to the Cure song, "Seventeen Seconds." So I can't pretend that Raymond, you know, corrupted me.

He started picking me up at World Sight almost every day. He waited outside on the white stone plaza and we went to Glide and to Shelby's and to Denzi's. We sat on the green benches in Central Park and it seemed that nothing bothered Raymond. I saw the flush on his skin and he was happy. He was content just to feel the breeze on his skin, while I was always waiting for something.

'So tell me about Beck,' he said one night.

'Beck? He's a corrections officer.'

'A corrections officer? Jesus.'

'What's wrong with that?'

'He must be an asshole.'

'Don't say that.'

'What are you doing with a corrections officer?'

I shook my head. He had no business talking about my private life. He had no business saying anything.

I started to walk off, but he followed me. 'Oh, come on,' he pulled at me. 'Let's get a drink.'

※

Sometimes things just happen all around you, and they happen fast—the way in Antigua, in January, the sun set so suddenly that we hardly noticed it, Raymond and Eric and I, and then it was dark, our mother on the porch ringing the dinner bell. It was nice to think that things could be different between Raymond and me. But Dr. Keats says this is where I fooled myself—that situations like the one I had with Raymond never just go away.

※

One night, it was summer by then, we were in my apartment, sitting at my table drinking from green bottles of beer. Above us was an African dance class, the sound of drums and sixty feet moving across the wood floor. 'Can I have some?' I finally asked.

'Some what?'

'Some of what you're doing.'

'Which is?'

I tilted my head to one side. 'Coke?'

He lit a cigarette, plucking a piece of tobacco from his tongue.

'I've done it before, Ray.'

'You have?'

People always think I am so innocent. Like this man Reese, who stopped me on the street once and asked me if I wanted to earn a lot of money—*a lot*, he said; he told me I had the face of a nun.

'Plenty of times,' I told Ray, 'in school.'

I went to the kitchen for more beer and when I came back, he had put out two lines for me.

'Thank you,' I said.

'You're welcome.'

He took a sip of his beer.

'So,' he said, 'have you seen anyone since Beck?'

'A few people.'

In Antigua, Ray had had a girlfriend called Alison. They had been like one person, drinking beer from one bottle, eating fish and chips from one packet, their house littered with her clothes and his, with teacups and ashtrays and newspapers. She worked as a nurse's aide. She lost her job for stealing prescription pads and letting Ray forge them.

'So what are you going to study in the fall?' I asked Raymond.

'I don't know. Psychology. Marine biology.'

Ray had spent hours at Pigeon Point, searching rock-pools for starfish and crabs. Once he dissected a crab and left it on my pillow. My father gave him a whipping for that. Then he left spiders in my shoes. He started humming a song, *I don't like spiders and snakes*, as he sidled along the walls of the house, *but that ain't what it takes to love me.*

⚞

The fact is, I tell Keats, Raymond had changed in the years he was away. He was solicitous now, courteous. He opened doors for me and paid for drinks for me and gave me his jacket if I was cold. He always answered when I called, came when I asked.

'So you cared for him,' Dr. Keats says.

'I didn't say that.'

'You let him into your life.'

'Yes—'

'So you cared.'

'Oh, *please*.' I get up from my chair, the way I am not supposed to. I shake my head at him and sort of raise my hand and then I am out the door, down the hall, into the parking lot.

Kenneth is there, leaning against the black Lincoln Continental. He has been a driver here for sixteen years. His hair is soft-looking and silver. He wears black Ray-Bans, black pants, and a black tie on a short-sleeved white shirt. His red and white Winston cigarette pack shows through his shirt pocket.

'Can I have one?' I ask.

'Sure.'

The flame from his lighter sizzles around the cigarette paper. It doesn't taste good, though. My mouth is too dry.

'Going for a swim today?'

'Maybe.'

Keats comes out of the doctors' office, smiling at me as if I haven't just walked out on him. 'That your doctor?' Kenneth asks.

'Yes.'

'Young guy.'

⚞

By July, Ray and I weren't sleeping. We sat with the air conditioner on high, drinking beer and doing cocaine. We went to his dealer three and four times a night. I stayed outside with the building super, Jesus, and in five minutes Ray was back, his eyes gleaming dark and skittish, packets of cocaine in his socks.

Wayne sat me down on his couch at World Sight. I was drinking milky iced coffee, the sugar grainy at the bottom. 'What is it?' I smiled.

'You've lost some weight.'

Cocaine will do that, though I didn't say so. Instead I said, 'It's summer.'

'I sound like a parent, I know.' He ran his hand through his fine dark hair. 'It doesn't suit me, does it?'

I laughed.

'How is Ray faring?'

'Fine.'

'Is he using drugs?'

I shrugged.

'He never offered them to you, did he?'

I looked off at the East River, gray as a dirty coin. 'In high school, maybe.'

He shook his head. 'Asshole.'

'He's all right.'

'I should call your parents.'

He wouldn't, though. It seemed to me that Wayne was a little in awe of them. He was four years younger than my mother, eight years younger than my father, and everyone in their town had known them. Wayne didn't want to bring them bad news. He wanted to impress them—the way, for instance, when I was in high school, he always brought his dates to the house, as if for my parents' approval.

⁂

I got a letter from my mother today. Her name was printed at the top:

LAURA

Dear Betsy,

I hope the summer is as lovely in Kent as it is here. Last night the Chubbs came for dinner in the garden. The music school opened their windows and we had our own little opera performance. It was just about perfect, though of course we miss you. Eric loves Drama School and Raymond is visiting some friends out in Montana. Your father and I have to go to Boston for a few days, but you can always call on the cellular.

With love, your mother

I read this letter to Dr. Keats and he asks how it makes me feel and I say homesick.

'What about her telling you about Raymond?'

I shrug.

'They must know how you felt about him.'

'They know.'

'But they ignore it?'

They knew if I said 'Hello,' he said 'Hello.' If I said 'Stop it,' he said 'Stop it.' They knew he mimicked me, watched me, waited for me—that he tripped me up and pulled me, by the hair, by the arm, by the leg, down under the house onto the yellow soil as my mother called out, 'Raymond, Raymond.'

He'd leave me in the dust then, take off down the rough ragged cliffs to the beach while my mother called out, 'Get up, Betsy. Get up,' so I did.

'You encourage him,' she'd tell me off. 'You take the bait. He knows you'll take the bait, and if you don't, he'll stop.' But neither of us stopped.

'"*Thy brother came with subtlety*,"' I intone to Dr. Keats "'. . . *and hath taken away thy blessing*." Genesis, 31:35.'

Eric writes:

Dear Betsy,

It's sweltering here. There's no air-conditioning so everyone is in a bad mood. Last weekend I went to Nantucket. They were having a Swann yachting regatta, with a simultaneous display of Rolex watches and Rolls Royce's. It was pretty disgusting.

Henry sends a photograph of a field of tulips. We went to high school together.

Dear Betsy, my Bets, my Best, My Girl, my Friend,
I cannot believe you are in that place. Then again, maybe it is good for you? Please call me and let me know if I can visit.

Wayne sends letters scrawled on legal pads and stationery from hotels in Botswana and France, pages torn from notebooks and World Sight/Wayne Carter writing pads.

Dear Betsy,
Meet me upstairs?

But that was a long time ago.

Dear Betsy,
I felt so wretched when I saw you pass by my office today. I want so much for you to be happy, to find someone who can love you completely, as you deserve, someone your own age who can make you happy. But I just cannot give up on this idea of you, of you and me together.

This idea of me.

Dear Betsy,
Dear Betsy,
Dear Betsy,
Ida and I have taken a trip to Medemblik, a tiny fishing village on the North Sea. She is angry, of course, but more

hurt because I know and she knows, too, how much I long to be on another beach with you. Still I am committed to making our marriage work, and so is she. I wanted so much to make a life with you, but I just couldn't do it, couldn't stop the terrible feeling of wrongness. My only consolation is that perhaps now you can get some real help. I wish I could say something to give you hope about us, but it would be wrong. Be strong, move on in your life and don't look back. You have so much love in you, so much goodness and courage. My thoughts race to you and my heart breaks.

'Kenneth?' I ask, in the doctors' office parking lot.

He is leaning against the black Lincoln. 'Yes?'

'May I use your lighter?'

He passes it to me. I hold up the letter in its envelope and set the edge on fire. I watch it burn, pale yellow with a flicker of orange. When it scalds my fingers, I drop it to the tar.

And where is Wayne now?

In Belgium.

And where are you?

'Jesus, Jesus,' Kenneth says, stamping out the flaming letter with his black lace-up shoes. 'What are you doing?'

He calls for Dr. Keats on his transistor radio. 'They'll put you in Little House, you realize that?'

Little House—Acute House—house behind the doctors' office where the suicides are, where they watch you twenty-four hours a day, nurses sitting at the edge of your bed.

In a few minutes, Dr. Keats comes out.

'Oh, *please*,' I say.

'What's going on?'

The letter is in ashes on the lot.

'She set that letter on fire,' Kenneth says.

'Who was it from?'

'"There is a friend that sticketh closer than a brother."'

'Betsy.'

I am not religious. I just like the words of religion.

'Proverbs 18:24.' I flick Kenneth's lighter. 'You don't care,' I tell Keats. 'You're paid to care.'

'Call for Vicki,' Keats tells Kenneth.

I know what that means: more drugs.

'Who wrote the letter, Betsy?'

'It doesn't matter.'

Dr. Keats shakes his head. He runs his hand over his brow and I feel sorry for him, suddenly.

'Wayne wrote it,' I say. 'Wayne who is in *Medemblik* with *Ida*. Wayne who hopes that now I can get some *real* help.

'Asshole,' I say.

Vicki comes down and the sun is hot overhead. Dr. Keats rolls up his sleeves, his smooth blue unwrinkled sleeves, and everyone waits until I take my Haldol, liquid Haldol, swimming like Sambuca in a clear plastic cup.

PART II

I HAVE BEEN in Dobson House for two months. It is small and wood, painted white. Out back is a sun deck, three white plastic sun chairs facing the woods, tall dark trees tangled and woven together. In front is a porch with a brick ledge where Robbie and I play guitar. He is forty-three and an art dealer from Long Island. He wears red polo shirts that get sweat marks under the arms, from his detox.

My room is on the third floor, in the old attic. It has a single bed, a bureau, and a wooden chair. It has two square windows with screens. They don't allow cameras here, but I cut a picture of Keats from the Fairley newsletter. His skin is soft and smooth-looking. His hair is regular brown and his eyes are blue. I have a postcard of Fairley also, from the gift shop. I have a photograph Henry sent me of tulips in a field, blue and red and gold in the Brooklyn Botanic Garden where we went once.

The doctors' office is up the hill, next to Dining Hall and Main House. Keats is at the back, past Admissions. His shirt is pale blue, with the smooth light sheen of part polyester/part cotton. His tie is navy blue and loosely knotted. Out the window, the grass is thick and green and dark.

He sets a coffee cup on his desk. It is actually two cups, one inside the other. 'When did you first realize that you weren't doing well?'

'That would be with Beck.'

'Beck?'

'Beck and Frank.'

'Which was when?'

'When Raymond left.'

'Six years ago. Let's start there.'

Ray was twenty-one and I was fifteen and he had been home for three weeks. In one more, he was going back to Antigua. Before that, though, he was at home, in his room. We shared the top floor. His room was on the garden, large and dark and painted navy blue. Mine was on the street with red brick walls and a red shag rug and a gymnastics bar hanging from the ceiling.

Sylvia came over after school. She was lying on my bed, in one of her vintage dresses and shiny new black riding boots. I was at my desk in my swivel chair. Raymond came in, in his usual outfit; black jeans and a black T-shirt and a black shirt. His feet were bare because he never went out.

'Who's your friend?' he asked me.

Sylvia turned onto her side on the bed. Her hair was long and yellow blond, wavy like ribbons. 'Sylvia,' she said.

'Hello, Sylvia. I'm Raymond.'

'Hello, Raymond.'

They spoke so slowly, they looked at each other so my muscles ached. They ached in my arms and my shoulders and my chest.

'What do you want?' I asked.

'Just looking.'

I got up from my chair and went to him. His eyes were the color of dark asters.

I tried to close the door but he held it open with his foot.

'You didn't have to be mean,' Sylvia said when he was gone.

'You don't even know him.'

'Maybe I'd like to.'

'Maybe you wouldn't.'

'Isn't he going away again? To another school?'

'To Antigua.'

'Well, then.'

I walked her home: up Madison Avenue to 79th Street and Fifth. It was autumn and the store windows shone like mirror and traffic lights glowed inside them. People were wearing new fall coats and a breeze was rising cool as an eddy in dark water.

'You never talk about him,' Sylvia said.

'About who?'

'Ray.'

'So.'

'He's good-looking. As good-looking as Eric.'

'Sylvia.'

'What?'

'I don't talk about your brother.'

I left her at her building and walked east. I didn't like people coming over when Ray was there. I stood on Lexington and 79th Street, waiting for the light to change. That's when I saw someone looking at me. He had close, almost shaved hair and his arms were crossed over a white T-shirt. He had big muscles, as if from weight-lifting.

'Hey,' he said.

He was leaning against a car, and he didn't look like the kind of boy who would speak to me. He was too good-looking and he was Raymond's age and he didn't look like he went to school or even worked anywhere.

'I'm Beck,' he said, pushing off the car, walking over to me. 'Beck Thomas Delaney.'

The light changed.

I smiled at him the way you might smile at someone on a bus. I started walking and he walked beside me, moving around parking meters and people and traffic signs to stay in step with me.

'What's your name?'

'Betsy.'

Even then, he looked like someone in the Marines; his face was all hard bones: strong jaw, strong forehead. He had freckles on his cheekbones.

'I've seen you,' he said. 'I've seen you before.'

He didn't even have a jacket.

'You have a friend, don't you? With blond hair.'

'Yes.'

He wanted to meet her. Lots of guys wanted to meet Sylvia.

'I wanted to talk to you, but you were always with her.'

I glanced sideways at him.

'You're not from here, right?'

'No.'

'See, I knew it. I told this friend of mine, I just bet you were from somewhere else.'

He was so excited. I started to laugh.

'You're from the country, right?'

'Antigua.'

'Antigua, shit. Don't mind my ignorance.'

Most people didn't know where Antigua was. Most just pretended. 'It's this little island,' I explained, 'in the Caribbean.'

'British, right?'

'Yes.'

'Wow. Shit. I'm glad I talked to you, Betsy. I really am.'

He seemed nice. He was polite.

On my block, we stopped outside Eat Here Now. Inside, an old woman in a blue raincoat was eating rice pudding with a long silver spoon.

'You want some?' Beck asked.

'No, thank you.'

'I'll buy you some.'

'No, really.'

'You're going to leave me now? We just met and you're going to leave?' He had an accent, the kind of New York accent I only heard on TV.

'I live here.'

'Right here? Or down the street?'

'Down the street.'

'Where do you go to school?'

I shouldn't tell him. I shouldn't have even spoken to him, a stranger on the street.

He took hold of my shirtsleeve with his finger and his thumb. He held onto the white edge of it.

'Houghton,' I said.

'Houghton?'

'You know it?'

'Sure.'

* * *

At midnight, the light from the streetlamp made a line across my room. I heard a siren on Lexington. I heard a car outside idling. I heard Ray's door and then the bathroom door and then tap water running in the sink. *I don't like spiders and snakes,* Ray was humming, using his special acne soap, *but that ain't what it takes to love me.*

The next day, Beck was at school, leaning against a car again, his arms folded on his white T-shirt. 'Betsy,' he said. 'What're you doing?'

'Nothing.'

He pushed up off the car. He came and stood close to me, closer than he had in the street. 'I was up all night,' he said, so quiet no one else could hear him. 'All night, thinking about you.'

I laughed. 'You were not.'

Sylvia came out, raising her eyebrows at me. 'You ready?' she asked. Henry was with her, lagging behind.

Beck nodded his head, motioning for me to step to the curb with him. 'You going somewhere with her?'

'Yes.'

He smelled warm. He smelled of mints. ''Cause you can just tell me if I'm bothering you.'

'You're not.'

'I mean, you know—' he looked down 91st Street '—you're like this beautiful thing.'

I was not beautiful. I was beautiful enough, my mother said.

'You know where PS 6 is, on 81st Street? I'm there, every day after four. You can find me there.'

'Okay.'

Henry winked at me. His hair was soft and fine like a child's. His black cashmere scarf was starting to pill. We watched as Beck turned and waved to me, heading down to Lexington.

'Who was that?' Henry asked.

'Beck.'

'Beck? Like the singer Beck?'

Sylvia rolled her eyes. They were the color of caramel.

'Where does he go to school?' Henry asked.

'I don't know. I just met him.'

'Henry—' Sylvia said, pushing him with one hand on the chest, kissing him at the same time on the mouth. 'Bye.'

'Wow,' she said as we walked down Lexington. 'He's got attitude, hasn't he? Like, this don't-mess-with-me thing.'

'Beck?'

'Where'd you meet him?'

'On the street.'

'The street? Jeeze, Betsy.'

'I know. He just started talking to me. Then he walked me home. He was nice.'

'He doesn't go to private school.'

'How do you know?'

'You can tell. I mean, his hair. Those sneakers. The way he stands.' She shrugged. 'Not that that's bad.'

Sylvia and her parents lived on 79th and Fifth. They had a penthouse, white marble with a white foyer and white living room and hallway. The carpet had vacuum lines on it.

'Hello, Mother,' Sylvia said, in the kitchen.

She was in a white nightdress and robe, drinking tea. Her hair was short and blond and spiky.

'Hello, darling. Did you have a good day?'

'It was okay.'

'Betsy?'

'Yes, thank you.'

'There are grapes,' she said. 'And strawberries.'

'Thank you. Thank you, *eely tentacle*. Are you going out tonight?'

'Not till ten.'

Sylvia's mother shuffled off in her white spongy slippers.

Sylvia's room was like a hotel suite: It had its own hallway with a door that locked. It had a double bed, a brown velvet couch, and matching chairs. She lay on her couch with her riding boots on. 'Pass me a Coke.'

I took one from her mini-fridge. 'I can't believe you called your mother an eely tentacle.'

Sylvia shrugged. She had been named after Sylvia Plath. 'Medusa,' she told me, '*Ariel*. She's heard it before.'

'Where are they going after ten o'clock?' I asked.

'Regine's, probably, dancing with the orthodontist.'

'What orthodontist?'

'My old one. He goes there, too.'

'Do you ever go with them?'

'No.'

We went out with our parents, Eric and Ray and I. We went to plays, mostly, and the movies.

From the couch, Sylvia's hair fell to the floor, just brushing the dark brown carpet. 'I have something for you.'

'Do you?'

'Oh, yes.'

I raised my eyebrows.

'By my bed.'

Her brother Sean was in boarding school and sometimes sent her cocaine. It came in envelopes made from the pages of magazines. I found one at the back of Sylvia's nightstand. Sylvia tapped it out on her coffee table, cutting it extra fine with a razor blade. We drank Cokes and listened to Neil Young.

'How's Henry?' I asked.

'A bore.'

'No—' I said, 'not really?'

'We have sex all the time. It's not healthy.'

⚸

Once, before Raymond left, I went into his room. It was large and dark and on the garden. Green leaves stuck to the bottom of the windowpanes. The carpet was rough and blue and worn shiny in patches. On the floor, a pile of CDs had gathered dust, old ones that belonged to my parents: Simon & Garfunkel and José

Feliciano. Above the desk was a photograph of Raymond and Eric smoking cigars at L'Hotel Oiseau in Paris. There was a picture of some kids from his school—I didn't know which because he had been to a few, but the girls had long hair and down jackets and peasant skirts, so maybe it was the Berkshires.

In his desk was an empty packet of Rothmans cigarettes, postcards from Key West and Paris and Los Angeles.

Dear Raymond

Dear Raymond

Dear Raymond

BACCI, one girl wrote at the end of every card, instead of a name.

There was a packet of pictures from Antigua. I wasn't in any of them.

The next day, the day after Beck came to school, Ray left for Antigua. My parents made Eric and me stay home. Ray wasn't allowed out, so he and Eric played billiards in the basement. I kept to my room, mostly, rearranging pictures and postcards on my wall.

For lunch, we ordered in burgers and fries from Eat Here Now. We didn't sit together, because Ray was busy getting packed. Afterwards, Dad went into Ray's room and shut the door. I was trying to read *The Basketball Diaries,* only I could never concentrate when Dad went into Ray's room. Sometimes they fought and I didn't like to hear it. Or maybe I did. Finally, Dad went out and downstairs and I realized that Ray would be coming out soon, with all his things, so I went down ahead of him. We had said goodbye to Raymond about five times now. Maybe it was normal, but I had noticed that every time someone was going away, everyone else became especially nice. We all stood around the cab, piling Ray's suitcases in, and at first Dad was his usual self, slightly sarcastic, slamming down the lid to the trunk and saying, 'It's your life.' Ray was wearing a red and white checked shirt my mother had given him once. He had showered and shaved and it was a super bright clear day, all the streets washed clean and the sky fresh like a wet painting. Dad shook Ray's hand and then put his arm around him, whispering something, and Ray nodded, his eyes on the pavement.

'Say goodbye to Ray,' Dad said, so Eric and I shook his hand. Then my mother hugged him. Finally, when he got in the cab, in his checked shirt to try to please my mother, in his black jeans and boots, it was as if, just for a moment, we actually were sad that he was leaving, so Ray rolled down his window, leaning out to prolong the departure.

'Well, there it is,' Dad said, memorializing in advance, as the cab rounded the corner. My mother hardly ever cried, but when she did her eyes went almost lavender-colored and no one could talk to her. She went up the stairs, to her room, probably, Dad still looking out toward the cab even after it turned the corner. Finally he asked, 'What are you up to, Eric?'

Eric was twelve then and into everything: chess, soccer, math. 'Practice,' he said.

'Betsy?'

'I guess I'll go to Sylvia's.'

Dad was going to his club, which was on the way to Sylvia's, so I walked him up Park Avenue. A breeze was tossing around dry leaves in the gutters and neither of us spoke. His club was on 68th Street, and he played squash there, and backgammon. We went for dinner sometimes, in a dining room with crimson coxcomb and portraits of the founders on the wall. One night my father had taken me down to the games room in the basement. The floor was white and black in great stone slabs, the sofas and chairs lacquered red. Two men were playing cards at a table, their jackets undone so you could see their cumberbunds.

'No women,' one of them said, jumping up when he saw me. He had a cigar in one hand. His eyes were bright gritty black, like stones at the bottom of a river.

My father laughed. 'Oh, so sorry,' he said, in this mocking way he had. He pulled me back to him, covering my eyes with his hand, the way he did at the movies, during sex scenes.

* * *

I thought of going to Sylvia's. I really did. I walked up Madison Avenue and the sky was blue as a baptism and *Raymond was gone,* I thought. Raymond was gone and would not come back. Happiness spread out in me like warm weather. I stood at the telephone outside Sylvia's. I lifted the receiver and put it down. I walked uptown to 81st Street, and turned left. By then, the sun had gone. I stood on the sidewalk in my corduroys and white shirt and boots, doing up the zipper on my jacket. The schoolyard was fresh with tar, the basketball court lit with streetlamps so the white painted lines gleamed. The sidewalk shone with flecks of glass, and Beck was running backwards down the court, in his green fatigues and T-shirt. He was like this great force, so confident and strong. He moved the whole time, never stopping, never showing anything on his face. Then when he saw me, he stopped in his tracks. I saw myself enter him, saw the moment his brain recognized me, and it was amazing, because his whole face, which had been expressionless until then, just started to shine, his smile like this beautiful thing—which is what he'd called me. On the court was Tommy, tall and lanky with dirty blond hair. There was Seth, heavyset, his skin pale and pockmarked on his cheeks. Beck dropped the basketball from his hand, flicking it behind him, so Tommy picked it up, turning it over in his long hands. They all called after him, but Beck didn't look back. There was just him and me, and when he reached me, he touched my hair. 'Hey, beautiful,' he said. 'What are you doing?'

My hands made fists in my pockets. I moved them up and down. 'I came to see you.'

'No shit.' He wiped his forehead on his sleeve. 'I didn't think you would.'

'No?'

'I'm flattered, I really am.'

My hands were sweaty.

There was a girl on the bench, her hair thin and blond, her legs solid in tight denim jeans.

'Let's go somewhere,' Beck said.

We went to Central Park. The leaves were orange and yellow and red. A breeze turned them over, like cards.

'You been at school?'

'No.'

'No?'

'My brother went away today.'

'Yeah? Where to?'

'Antigua.'

Down at the boat pond, the benches shone with new coats of green paint. Two old women in fur hats were eating ice cream. Their mouths were small with pink lipstick.

'Sit here,' Beck said. 'No, not there, here.' I sat on his legs. They were warm from basketball. I put my hand on his shoulder, to balance myself. 'My mother's from Iceland.'

'Is she?'

'Yeah. It's not even icy there. It's green.'

'Antigua is green—green and also blue.'

'Like your eyes.'

'Yes.'

'Your eyes are blue.'

His eyes were the color of dry grass in summertime.

He put his arm around my lower back. 'You like your brother?'

'Not much.'

He laughed. Patches of light shone on the pond water.

'How many brothers do you have?'

'Two.'

'No sisters?'

'No.'

'Two parents?'

'Yes.'

'I don't have any of that. No brothers. No sisters. No father. Just my mother. She's a waitress.'

'That's nice,' I said.

He laughed. '*That's nice*,' he repeated, and tightened his grip.

'It's not so nice.'

'I'm sorry.'

'You're like—a *girl*, you know that?'

'I am a girl.'

'Not the kind I know.'

'What kind do you know?'

'I don't know. Girls who wear makeup and shit, who are always brushing their hair.'

'I brush my hair.'

'You have nice hair.'

'Thank you.'

My hair was my best feature, according to my mother, long and dark and straight.

'The first time I saw you, it was like—' he held a hand to his chest, 'my heart stopped.'

'It did not.'

'It did. I felt it.'

'You did not.'

'Right here.'

We started laughing then. He was so close to me, his warm skin, his full slightly bruised-looking mouth. I bent backwards, him holding me by the small of my back, my hair almost touching the ground, the red and yellow leaves damp, translucent, pasted to the ground as if with clear liquid glue.

'Beck Thomas Delaney,' I smiled, sitting up, breeze shifting through the tops of the trees. I slipped off his legs onto the bench.

'Yes.'

He watched me like I was a kid.

'Where do you go to school?' I asked.

'Me?'

'Yes.'

'Oh, man.' Something light left his face and something else came into it. He took a packet of Marlboros from his jacket and lit one. 'You shouldn't ask.'

'Why not?'

''Cause I don't go to regular school, Betsy.' He blew smoke above his head, into the trees. 'I go—I don't want to scare you—I go to Correctional School. You know what that is?'

'Yes.'

'You do?'

'Yes.'

* * *

Raymond had been in Correctional School in Antigua. It was in St. John in an old courthouse, whitewashed, two stories high. Around it was a yellow lawn, scrubby with a black iron fence. We went to visit one Sunday, sitting at the picnic benches out back, the ash wooden planks bleached and split from the sun. My mother set out ham sandwiches and pint-sized cartons of chocolate milk. 'Everyone's staring,' she said. She often thought people were staring. Maybe they were.

'Not that I have to,' Beck said. 'I mean, I've done my time. It's over. I'm clean. I can walk. But I didn't, you know. I stayed on 'cause I want to learn.'

'That's good.'

'Yeah.'

He dropped his cigarette. We watched as a puddle soaked it brown. 'Now you won't talk to me,' he said, 'right?'

His hair looked soft as a cat's pelt.

'I'll talk to you.'

'Will you?'

'Sure.'

He kissed me then. It was like when leaves start rushing in the trees above you. It was like that, only in my chest.

When I got home, Raymond's plane was taking off. My mother came to her door, her face swollen from crying.

'Where have you been?' she asked.

'Nowhere.'

I smelled of Beck and the park and cigarette smoke.

'Nowhere?'

'No.'

She waved her hand and closed her door, starting to cry again.

✿

Besides my hair, my mouth is a good feature. My upper lip is arced like a crescent. My body is angular and thin. My favorite part is the hipbone when one leg crosses the other on the bed, the bone under my skin rounded and smooth. I have a soft stomach, also, like the insides of my thighs. My feet are a size too big, as are my hands. My breasts are not large, but not flat; they are rounded. I like large shirts. Dad likes to take photographs of me, and in most of them my shoulders are hunched forward. I am laughing, because Dad likes me most when I laugh, my hair combed straight and sleek across my back.

✧

My mother started volunteering at the Whitney Museum, every afternoon from three until six. My father went to his club and Eric was always at school at one of his clubs or games.

Each day, Beck left for school at 6:51 a.m. on the MetroNorth train from Grand Central. His school was called Hawthorne and was somewhere near Peekskill. He came back at 3:05, took the express to 86th Street, and waited for me outside Houghton. He stood out the way some street kid would, tough and a little awkward, arms on his chest. He smoked a cigarette, maybe, or drank an orange soda, not smiling at anyone but me.

We went to the schoolyard, Tommy and Seth and their friends on the court. Beck pulled me to his chest from behind, his arm around my shoulders. *'I love you baby,'* he sang in my ear, *'and if it's quite all right, I need you baby.'* He got down on his knees, so I laughed. 'You kill me,' he said, putting his fist to his chest. 'Right in here.'

On Sheep's Meadow, the lawn smooth and cool, we went into the middle and lay out. 'Look.' He dangled his keys in the air before me, on a metal ring.

'Yes?'

'We could go to my house.' His sweater was blue wool, crewnecked. 'You want to?'

'No.'

'Don't you trust me?'

I didn't know.

'Here,' he said. He took a photograph from his wallet. It was a woman, her hair brown and parted in the middle. 'This is my mother.' He showed me an old picture, creased and grayed and grimy at the edges. 'My dad.' He didn't look like Beck. He was tall and slim and smiling, standing in front of a plane.

'Was he a pilot?'

'He was just standing there.'

He had this great smile, a fake all-out smile, his shirt white and open at the neck.

'Now you know everything.' He flipped the keys on the ring. 'Trust me now?'

'Why did they put you in Correctional?'

''Cause I was bad. 'Cause I did some shit.'

'What does that mean?'

'It means, like, I was bad news. I kind of was bad news, Betsy.'

'What's the worst thing you did?'

'Oh shit, I don't know.'

His sweater had a loose thread at the cuff. I pulled at it.

'Don't,' he said.

'I'm sorry.'

'That's a new sweater.'

Over by the high trees, a man was playing a harmonica. His jacket was down, cobalt blue and puffy. My father played the harmonica. He played the guitar, also. He played 'Stewball' and 'Mack the Knife' and 'Banks of the Ohio.'

'What's your favorite song?' I asked.

'I don't know. I like that song—what's it called? "Ain't No Use in Crying."' He took out his cigarettes. 'We should go to my house.'

'No.'

He shook his head. 'Betsy.'

'What?'

'Betsy, Betsy.'

'Stop saying that.' I lay back on the grass. It was cool and soft. When he kissed me, his mouth was warm.

'Jesus,' he said.

'What?'

'You.'

He put his finger in my mouth. It was dry and salty.

The man with the harmonica was using his jacket as a big blue pillow.

'You want to know my favorite song?' I asked.

'What?'

'*Old Stewball was a racehorse, and I wish he were mine. He never drank water, he always drank wine.*'

'*Stewball*? What kind of name is that?'

'I don't know. It's a song. My Dad used to play it.'

Beck and Tommy went to Correctional, Seth was out of school, and Sharon went to Wagner High. I spoke to her once. Her earrings had tiny Jesuses crucified. She had dark eye shadow and told me she liked the way I spoke. 'You're so quiet,' she said.

'Not really.'

'Don't people tell you that?'

'Sometimes.'

She picked at a cuticle with a fingernail. 'Well, you are.'

The schoolyard was empty at dusk, streetlamps blurred yellow at the edges, dust on the green benches. Tommy sat in his army jacket, his knees up. His eyes were like great shiny pools of water, the pale blue of marbles. He lived in Queens, Beck said, his mother was on welfare, and their place was 'the worst in the world.' Seth was eating french fries and wiped the grease on his leather jacket.

'Hey,' Beck said. 'Don't fucking do that.'

Seth stopped with his hand in the box. 'What?'

'It's disgusting, wiping that shit on yourself.'

Seth put more french fries in his mouth. 'Where'd you get her?' he asked, his fingers greasy. 'I mean it. Where'd you find her?'

Tommy laughed, dropping his head in his lap, wrists hanging loose over his knees.

'Fuck you, man,' Beck said. 'Both of you. Come on,' he then said to me, getting up.

We bought coffee with milk and sugar and took it to the steps of the Met. The museum was still open, people going up and down the steps in their high-heeled boots and their rubber soles. The sky was navy blue, the lights on the fountain white.

'What do you want to do,' I asked, 'after school?'

'I don't know. I can't write. I can hardly read. What am I going to do? Be a doctor? A lawyer?' It was the first time I'd heard him that way, bitter.

'You can read.'

'I read like a nine-year-old. That's what they told me.'

'You're smart.'

'Yeah, well, it doesn't matter. 'Cause I already know. I'm going to join the Marines.'

I didn't know anyone who wanted to be a Marine.

'If they'll take me,' he said, 'which they won't because of my record.'

'Will they take you if you graduate?'

'That's the plan.'

'What do they do?'

'The Marines? They're the best. The toughest, the strongest, the first to fight. And—I could get out of here. I've never been anywhere. I've never been out of New York.'

'Really?'

'Yeah.'

'You've never been overseas?'

'No.'

'To the ocean?'

'No.'

I picked at the seam on my leather glove. 'Can you swim?'

'After the Marines, I'll be able to swim.'

'What does your dad do?'

'My dad.' He laughed. 'He never even married my mother.'

'But he lives here?'

'They met in Iceland. He was on business or something. Then she followed him over.' He shrugged. 'Not that he wanted her to.'

He came to school, and it was a clear bright day with cold sliding in like currents. He stood below the windows, Tommy beside him in his loose green army coat. 'Yo, Betsy!' Beck called out. 'Betsy!' I was in English class.

Miss Porter went to the window. 'Is that for you, Betsy?' she asked me.

I got up and went to look and so did everyone else, and Beck had his arms crossed, his head thrown back and looking up.

'Impatient, isn't he?'

Then the headmaster went outside and I saw Beck step away from Tommy, over to the headmaster, so he shook his hand, the two of them talking, and then the bell went for the end of the day and Miss Porter laughed at me because she liked me and I took off into the hallway and down six flights of steps to the sidewalk where Beck was.

'What did you say to him?' I asked.

He had his hand in my hair. 'I said I had the impression that school got out at three.'

'Charming men are the worst kind,' Sylvia said. 'My dad told me. At the investment bank, he said, they're the ones that get the best of you—so you don't even notice.'

'What are you talking about?' Henry said. His hair was brown and so were his eyes and nothing about him was remarkable except that it was all perfect, not a flaw on him.

'He's mean. Then when *she* comes along he's Mr. Nice and Sweet.'

'He doesn't know anyone.'

'He's seen me with you.'

'You're just upset,' Henry said, 'because he doesn't speak to you.'

'He'd speak to me, if I wanted him to.'

Henry laughed, so Sylvia went inside to get more wine. Henry lived on Gracie Square, above the East River. His mother was a jazz singer, Miss Beth Rule Peake, and his father owned newspapers. He knew everything, Henry said, except about singing, which was why his mother could marry him.

It was cold on the terrace, the wind tumbling across the water and the moon almost full.

'What do you see in Beck anyway?' Henry asked, leaning over the railing in his long black scarf. 'Besides the obvious.'

'What's the obvious?'

'The way he looks.'

'He's nice.'

'Really?'

'Yes.'

'Isn't he in reform school?'

'Yes.'

His face was pretty like a girl's, soft lips and clear skin. 'So what do you talk about?'

I laughed. We didn't need to talk—Beck and I—the way he always saw me coming, the way he ran down the sidewalk and across the street, grinning and picking me up, kissing my throat, my lips, my neck.

'With her killer graces,' Beck sang, *'and her secret places, that no boy can fill . . .* You know who that is?'

'Who?'

'With her hands on her hips and that smile on her lips because she knows that it kills me.'

'Stop it,' I said.

He kissed my temple. 'Springsteen. "She's The One."'

'You're crazy.'

He pushed my hair aside. He smelled of smoke.

'Let's go to my house.'

'No.'

'You kill me, you know that?'

'We could go to mine.' He put his arm around me.

'Really?'

'Maybe.'

'Are your parents home?'

'I don't think so.'

The sky was infused with light, the way it is at dusk or the peak of the day. People looked at us as we walked, or at Beck. You're good looking, too, Sylvia told me. But not like Beck I wasn't.

Inside the house it was dark. The hallway smelled of freesia. In the kitchen, I poured Beck a soda, and everything looked different with him there. He looked different, sipping from a glass with cubes of ice.

'Nice,' he said in the living room, setting his glass on the coffee table.

I wasn't supposed to have anyone over. It was the first time we'd been alone in a room. Everything was quiet. Beck looked at the paintings and the blue couch and the silver candlesticks. He picked up a photo from the fireplace mantel. 'Who's this?'

'My mother.'

'She's pretty—and this?'

'Our house in Antigua.'

'It's on the sea?'

'Yes.'

'Is that your pool?'

'Yes.'

My parents had had the first swimming pool in Antigua. It took months to dig, workers grinding their jackhammers into the yellow earth of the dry hillside, pouring concrete from great trucks, sanding it and painting it blue, gluing on the white and blue porcelain tiles my mother had shipped from Italy. They had had the first pool party, except for the club at Mill Reef, all the staff in uniforms serving drinks and hors d'oeurves of oyster and tinned meat.

'What does your dad do?'

'He's a lawyer.'

'No shit. You never told me that.' He sat on the couch, propping himself on the edge, holding his hands between his knees.

'I didn't?'

'Lawyers fucking hate me, Betsy. They hate me.'

'Why would they?'

'I don't know. They just look at me. They hate me. Where's your room?'

'Upstairs.'

'Can I see it?'

'No.'

'You know how big our place is?'

'How big?'

'As big as this room—the whole place.'

He fished out a cube of ice from his glass. 'You know what my father did? When I was nine? We went to court in this paternity suit, right? Because he wouldn't pay child support. We had to take these tests, to prove he was my dad, and even after the tests said he was—even then—he said I wasn't. He looked me right in the eye and said, "That's not my son."'

I felt bad for him when he said that. I felt bad mostly because he did, because he carried that picture in his wallet.

'I'm sorry.'

'Yeah—well.' He set down his glass. 'My mother was fucking sorry. I tell you that.'

'Now?' Beck asked, pulling my hips into his, against a car by the playground. 'Now?' he asked, fingers in my long hair. We crossed the baseball diamonds, walking down to Dog Hill where it began to rain, the sky pale gray and misty, Beck balling up his jacket beneath my head so everything ran with water—the rain and his cheekbones and his hands.

'People are watching.'

'No, they're not.'

'They could be.'

He laughed. His mouth was wet with rain.

'Come on,' I said.

'What?'

'I'll go with you. To your house.'

'You will?'

He smirked and smiled at the same time, not wanting to look too pleased, I could tell, but pleased anyway, practically blushing, taking my hand and kissing it. 'All right,' he said, and we ran, all the way down Fifth Avenue, past the Pierre Hotel and Trump Plaza, left onto 53rd, where Beck hailed a cab, both of us out of breath, slamming the door and laughing. He lived on 32nd Street, in a tenement building. The hallway was dark chocolate brown, the stone steps worn down.

'Where's your mother?' I asked as Beck stood behind me at his door, dark door with no light in the hall.

'Working.'

'Is she coming home?'

'No.'

The hallway was narrow, the carpet thick and blue. On the right was the kitchen, a bottle of Crisco oil in the sink. The living room was on the street, with a view of a bare tree. I could smell cigarettes and something old, like flower water.

'Sit down.'

He turned on a glass lamp. The couch was blue velour like a sweater Eric had in Antigua. When I sat, it sank beneath me.

'Beck,' I said, wanting him to sit next to me.

'What?'

There was a big TV and a porcelain dog and a painting that looked like it had been done on black velvet, the kind of painting you see in dime stores.

'You want to see my room?' he asked, raising his eyebrows at me.

My palms made print marks on the coffee table.

It wasn't like a real room. There was no window. He had a bedside lamp, but didn't turn it on. The light came from the hallway, from its fluorescent bulb.

His carpet was strewn with clothes. 'Come here,' he said, sitting on his bed. I stood before him. He put his hands on my waist. His fingers where they touched my skin were cool.

'Are you nervous?'

'Yes.'

'I don't want to fuck you up.'

I put my arms around his neck. 'You don't?' I laughed.

We lay back on the sheets, which were dark green and flannel. He had one pillow, thin and flat.

'I don't like pillows,' I said.

'Everyone likes pillows.'

His skin was pale in the white light.

'Is your mother coming home?'

'No.'

'Can you close the door?'

'No.'

He kissed my mouth. His chest lay heavy on mine.

'Beck.'

'What?'

I moved my hands under his T-shirt. His skin was smooth.

'You have a nice mouth.'

When he kissed me, it was like I became him. It was a relief, like going into the ocean after you've been looking at it for a long time, wanting to.

He took off his T-shirt and then his pants were undone. He started rubbing himself, the way Raymond did. He moved his hand fast, not even looking at me. He pushed up my shirt and held onto my breast.

As when a storm comes, the sky empty one minute, dark the next, so a chill came over me. He came onto my stomach. His breath was hard and raspy, the sound of moths. I listened to him breathing. Then he wiped me off with his T-shirt.

'Are you okay?'

I wasn't, actually.

'I've got to go,' I said.

'Right now?'

It was the way it was with Raymond, the same exact way, once things were over.

At the door, he took hold of my shoulder, standing with his pants done back up but his chest still bare. 'Are you all right?'

'Yes.'

'Don't get fucking weird on me.'

He should have walked me out. He should have walked me home or put me in a cab. I wouldn't have let him, though, not even if he tried.

'What the hell was that?' he asked the next day, stepping in beside me after school, from the black gates to Lexington and down the street. 'Are you angry at me?'

I wouldn't look at him.

'You can't do that, Betsy. You can't just not say anything . . .
So I fucked up. Did I fuck up? What did I say? What did I do?'

'I can't say.'

'Yes, you can.'

'If you don't know . . .'

'That's bullshit. That is fucking bullshit.'

I stopped and turned to him. He was so upset. He couldn't be
bad, could he, if he were that upset?

'Okay,' I said, looking up the street, at the patch of blue sky
over the reservoir. 'It's okay. It's all right.'

The fact is, I was disgusted.

'Disgusted?' repeats Dr. Keats in his office.

'Yes.'

'That's a strong word.'

I shrug. 'It felt the same,' I tell him.

'The same as—?'

'As it did with Ray.'

'How so?'

'*The way of the wicked is dark and deep,*' I cite from the Bible
again.

Keats raises his eyebrows. 'You're not wicked.'

'We all are, don't you think?'

'What do you have after lunch?' Keats asks.

'Rec. Then Group.'

We didn't do anything again, after that. Or we did the usual,
lying around in the park, sitting on the stoop with his friends,
Beck picking me up and swinging me around upside down so
coins fell from my pockets.

Then Seth got a new car, shiny white with a gray modular
interior. He wanted me to sit up front with him, but Beck

wouldn't let me. 'He's rough with the ladies,' Beck whispered. 'Do you know what that means?'

'I think so.'

'Either you do or you don't.'

We went out to Queens one Saturday. I called Sylvia but she wouldn't come. 'No way,' she said. 'Call me later.' It was gray out, all the houses small and brick and in rows, plastic chairs on the porches. We pulled up outside a red brick house, a scraggly tree in the yard and cigarette butts in the grass.

Beck had the keys. Inside it was dusty and damp. Dust lay on the shiny wood floor, and the couches looked like furniture put out on the street. Beck brought in a case of beer from the car.

'Whose place is this?' I asked, standing in the kitchen.

'My dad's.'

'Your dad's?'

'He rents it out.'

He put the beer in the fridge. A packet of duck sauce had leaked onto the bottom. Tommy turned on an old television, on the floor against the wall. 'What happened to the fucking table?' he asked Seth.

'How do I know?'

'Fucking useless.' Tommy raised his eyebrows at me. He looked handsome sometimes. I liked his wavy hair and his eyes.

On the television, a talk show was on. 'I hate that shit,' Beck said. Tommy turned the sound off, taking a pipe from his jacket and sitting on a long couch the color of lavender. He unwrapped some tin foil. Inside was a square block, dry and brown like stale chocolate. He squeezed a piece into his pipe and winked at me.

'Want some?' he asked, lighting it. The smoke smelled sweet.

'Hey,' Beck said, stepping out of the kitchen. 'Don't fucking give her that.'

'All right,' Tommy said. 'Jesus.'

'Fucking prick,' Beck said. He went out to the car, shaking his head. When he came back, he had a bottle of vodka in his hand. He swung it by the mouth, between his fingers. He was so beautiful, I thought, in his navy blue sweater, frayed at the cuffs. 'All right, all right, give me that,' he said to Tommy and sat on the couch. He wouldn't let me have any, though. He poured me vodka in a coffee mug.

I didn't know what time it was after a while. The room was smoky, the curtains thin and gray, like shirts wet from washing. I had stretched out on the couch and Beck opened his eyes. 'How are you?'

'Okay.' His legs on mine lay hot as a cat.

'You're sure?'

'Yes.'

He picked up his beer bottle from the floor. Seth and Tommy were watching Jackie Chan, Tommy leaning back on his elbows, Seth cross-legged, ashtrays and beer bottles and packets of cigarettes between them. Beck undid a button on my shirt. It was a nice shirt, white with buttons like small pearls. I had bought it in England. 'Beck.'

'Yes?'

He moved his hand between my legs, touching me, so I smiled. He started kissing me, the kind of kissing you do when you have drunk too much so everything disappears. 'Beck,' I warned, the couch scratching my skin. 'Beck.' Then he came inside me. It hurt me for just a moment and then it was practically over.

Beck groaned, and it was a groan so obvious, Tommy and Seth started laughing. I pulled my body from under him. My foot knocked over an ashtray.

Outside, the fresh air made me dizzy.

I wanted to go home, to start walking and not look back. Where was I, though? And I hadn't brought my jacket, my money.

'Betsy,' Beck called, coming out onto the grass.

'What?'

'What are you doing?'

'Nothing.'

The sun was pale and hazy.

'You're just gonna wander around?'

I hated him then: his beautiful face, his cropped hair and bruised mouth and green fatigue pants.

'Why did you do that?'

'Christ, Christ, Betsy. I'm sorry. It just happened.'

I started crying. I never did anything right.

'Don't get crazy,' he warned.

'I'd like to go home.'

He swung his foot back and forth, scraping his clean white sneaker against the curb.

'All right,' he said, and turned back to the house. 'All right. I'll get the guys.'

Eric had been in *The Cherry Orchard* and *The Glass Menagerie* and now he was Puck in *A Midsummer Night's Dream*. I sat in the school theater and watched him rehearse, and he wasn't the way he was at home at all. He had all this energy. He laughed and moved around and talked to people. He was interested, the way he never was with me.

I walked down Third Avenue so I wouldn't run into Beck. I lay on my bed and watched the lights go on in the rooms in the brownstones across the street. The doorbell rang and my mother called up to me.

'Yes?' I could see her face, looking up at me from the ground floor.

'There's someone outside for you.'

''Who?'

'That Beck boy.'

'Can you tell him I don't want to see him?'

She said no. She said I wasn't to hide from anyone and if I didn't want to see him, I should tell him. I pulled on my boots and coat. 'Just tell him you're busy,' she called as I passed the kitchen, its dim reddish-yellow light and the smell of roast chicken.

Outside, it was cold. His face was washed out in the overhead light.

'What is it?' I asked, all cool the way my mother could be sometimes.

'You weren't at school.' I held the door open, just slightly, leaning on it with my back. 'Can't you come out?'

'No.'

He pulled my hand so I tilted forward slightly; the door shut behind me and he smiled, one of his smiles that changed his whole face, so I felt bad suddenly—him coming to see me and me just wanting to be rid of him.

It was dark, early in December, and already night. I kept my hands in my coat so he couldn't touch them. We crossed 64th Street into the park. A hot dog vendor was packing up his cart. A man in a double-breasted coat went up the stairs and smiled at me. We were near the zoo.

'Come on, Betsy,' Beck said. 'What is it? It's sex, right? You're upset about that.'

'Shouldn't I be?'

'I don't need sex from you. I can get that anywhere.'

'Can you?'

'Sure.'

I stepped toward him. 'From who? Sharon?'

He shrugged. There was a warm smell, of animals and dirt.

'You shouldn't have done that,' I said.

'I know.'

'Right in front of your friends.'

'I know.'

'Did you go out with Sharon?'

'Once or twice.'

'You did?'

'Don't be jealous.'

'Why not?'

He put his hands on my shoulders, glancing around as if someone might hear him.

''Cause I'm like—Betsy, I'm like sick from you.'

I looked away. 'You are not.'

'I can't fucking sleep for thinking of you. I told my *mother* about you. My fucking mother, Betsy.'

I smiled.

'I don't want to say that word, Betsy, 'cause it's the word I said when I was eight.'

'What word?'

He moved his face right close to mine. He was close enough

to kiss me. 'I love you.' He put a fist to his chest. 'Right in here, Betsy, right in here.'

He gave me the pill. I don't know where he got it, but it was a year's supply, a plastic canister and twelve packages. Sylvia laughed at me and said pills expired, pills were different for different people. We went down to Planned Parenthood and got new prescriptions.

At Christmas, Beck gave me a pair of earrings. Because they were diamonds, Dad said he wanted to meet Beck. 'Fuck,' Beck said, sitting on the bench at the playground, rubbing his almost-shaved head. 'Fuck, fuck, fuck.'

'He's nice. You'll like him.'

'I won't.'

'How do you know?'

'Because, Betsy, parents hate me.'

He came over after school, but my father was late. In the kitchen, my mother poured him a glass of orange juice and he moved his weight from foot to foot. He called my mother 'ma'am.' He said, 'Yes, ma'am,' and, 'No, ma'am,' and, 'Ma'am, you have a beautiful daughter—and I can certainly see why, if you don't mind me saying.'

'Not at all,' my mother said.

When Dad got home, we went into the living room. Beck and I were on the couch and Dad stayed at the fireplace, warming his hands behind his back. 'How old are you, Beck?' my father asked. His tie shone with flecks of silver, like flints.

'Twenty, sir.'

'Betsy is a little young to be getting diamonds.'

'Sir?'

I hated the way Beck said *Sir.*

'She's sixteen. She's in high school—as I'm sure you know— and we don't believe a girl her age should be wearing diamonds.' Beck didn't know what he was talking about. I didn't either, really, to tell the truth. 'I also understand that you met Betsy on the street.'

'Yes, sir, I did.'

'I'd rather you call the house in the future—if you want to see her.'

'Sir.'

'Also—and this is no offense to you, of course—but Betsy knows we don't like guests in the house when we're not here— Betsy's mother and I. You understand that, don't you, Betsy?'

'Yes.'

His cuff links were pale gray cotton knots. He had a set in navy also, and in pink.

'That's a lot of money for a boy in school to spend.'

'Not so much.'

'Perhaps you make more money than I do.'

'No, sir.'

My father laughed. 'It seems like a lot of money to me.'

'Not so much.'

'Are you still in school?'

'No, sir. I mean, I'm just about finished, sir. Hawthorne, upstate.'

'So you have a job?'

'Sometimes.'

'Sometimes.' My father laughed again. He took his hands from behind his back. 'Well, that's a good job.'

My father had wanted to be a judge, until Raymond was arrested. After all the publicity, though, he changed his mind. People came to Antigua on business or on charter yachts, and Dad invited them up to the house for cocktails and seared fish, fruit with brandy on the porch. They came by themselves or with their business partners or wives and children. They talked to Dad about Chicago and London and New York, and sometimes they offered him jobs, the last of which he took.

From the day he met him, Beck did what my father told him. He called from the street and from Grand Central and from his mother's at night. He took the telephone into the hallway outside the apartment, so his mother couldn't hear. I met him at the schoolyard or at Houghton, and other times he sent Tommy to pick me up. Tommy had a new girlfriend who was twenty-eight and lived in Queens and had an eight-year-old son. Her name was Deborah, Tommy said, pronouncing this 'Deb-OR-a.' He walked me downtown, or sometimes just to Seth's car, opening the door for me, closing it like a chauffeur, and singing, '*She's a rich girl, and she's going too far,*' so he and Seth started laughing.

I didn't want to go to Queens again. 'It's all right,' Beck said, putting his arm around me in the car. He was wearing his winter peacoat, too short at the sleeves when he raised his arms. 'Don't worry.'

'She should fucking worry,' Tommy said, so Beck pushed at his head from behind.

It had rained all morning: a cold drizzling rain turning the tree in the yard black. Seth plugged in a space heater that smelled of burning dust. In the kitchen, we had vodka in plastic cups, the ice cubes from the fridge grainy.

Beck put his finger in a loop of my cords. 'You should wear skirts.'

'Should I?'

'Skirts, heels, girly things.'

I loved his smile. I leaned up and kissed him. 'Come here.' He pulled me as Seth and Tommy prepared their hash. The floor was slippery under my socks.

'Where are we going?'

'Back here.'

There was a room next to the bathroom, one I had never seen. In it was a double bed, high off the ground with thin white sheets. At the window was a yellow curtain flapping.

When he kissed me, I heard rain and distant cars, the curtain flapping and Tommy laughing at the television.

'I want you to meet someone,' Beck said, lying beside me on the bed, elbow propping up his head.

'Who?'

'Remember the guy in the photograph?'

'Your dad?'

'Yes.'
'You want me to meet your dad?'
'Why not?'
Pale weak light hit the ceiling through the window.
'He lives downtown.'

PART III

I SAT IN the back with Tommy. Beck watched us in the rearview mirror, winking at me. His eyes were the clear light green of water in Antigua. On Mott Street, we walked into a red brick tenement, Beck close behind me, his palm on my back. There was a large wooden table and black folding chairs and two older men playing cards. I could smell beer. At the back of the room was a flight of stairs, unlit, concrete painted with thick gray enamel.

'Beck,' I said.

'What?' Everyone paused, stopping and surrounding me at the top of the stairs. On the radio a man and a woman were laughing. 'We're just saying hi.'

We went down the stairs, Beck with his hands on my shoulders.

'Dad,' he said. There was a man on a black couch, feet up on a coffee table. He was long and thin in the way of people who hardly bother to eat. His pants were black and pressed, his shirt white, his shoes expensive. His shirt was undone at the neck but had gold cuff links. When he looked at us, it was as if he hardly took us in, as if his eyes could hardly be bothered to settle.

'This here is Betsy.'

'Betsy what?'

'Scott.'

He had a cigarette in his left hand. Behind him were strings of red beads where a door should have been.

'Very pretty.'

'Thank you.'

'Nice pants.'

He had great blue eyes. He tapped his cigarette into an ashtray, the kind they sell at dime stores, red plastic with slots. Seth and Tommy moved to the refrigerator, opening bottles of beer.

'Come here,' Beck said. He took my forearm and sat me down between them.

Above his jawbone, the man had a slight scar, shiny and raised like a razor blade. He didn't move at all, not a fraction when I sat, and I got this feeling inside, suddenly, that something serious was going to happen, the way when the keel of a boat touches sand, you know you're going aground. *I don't like spiders and snakes,* came into my head, *but that ain't what it takes to love me.*

A drop of sweat ran down my side.

'What do you need?' the man said.

'Three hundred.'

He turned his eyes on me. They were deep and almost beautiful, but they didn't go with the rest of him.

'I want you to talk to Steve.'

'Now?'

'Soon.' He flicked ash from his cigarette into the red ashtray. 'So, where'd you two meet?'

'79th Street,' I said.

He laughed. '79th Street.' He circled his wrist so the bones cracked. He had a gold tank watch with gold links. 'What avenue?'

'Lexington.'

He stood up. 'Well,' he said, 'Dad'll be right back.' He went out the door. Beck wiped his forehead on his sleeve.

'That's not really your dad, is it?'

'No.'

'Why'd you say he was?'

He put his feet up on the table. 'I'm sorry.'

'Who is he?'

'Frank.'

The place I felt best was in Beck's room. It was dark. There was hardly any sound. Beck's body was smooth and also hard. I liked his chest, the hollow at the center and his slow heartbeat. He wrapped his legs around me, his hand on my bare back.

Beside his bed was a cigar box full of matchbooks and cigarettes, a hash pipe, and his beeper, which he didn't use. There was a picture of me on the porch of our Antigua house, *Stewball* moored in the bay. 'Where'd you get that?'

'Your house.'

'You took it?'

'Yeah.' He kissed me. His skin was warm and damp. 'That's your house, right?'

'It was.'

'I've never seen a place like that.'

'You should have asked me for it.'

'I know.'

He went to bars in Queens that he would never take me to. He went dancing, though I could not imagine him dancing. Some days, we'd be at the playground and Seth would drive up, Beck would go and talk to him, and sometimes he'd leave. Then Frank started coming, also. He had a silver Mercedes, which he kept idling at the curb. He smoked a cigarette out the window, sun on his gold link watch. It was like he didn't even see me, like he was thinking of something else and hardly noticed me. Then I realized that he did see me, he did notice me. He drove up in his car and I could feel him coming—the way you feel weather. I started to look for him—from the bench or the basketball court, or leaning against a car beside Beck.

'Hey, kiddies,' Frank would call, his eyes wide and dark and blatant.

Then one day, he got out of the car.

'Miss Scott.'

He was wearing a black leather blazer.

Beck looked at us from across the court, tossing the basketball from hand to hand.

'The boys treating you well?' He stood with his hands splayed on his hips.

'Yes.'

'You finished school already?'

'Three-thirty.'

'You don't have uniforms at your school?'

We had uniforms in Antigua. We had ties and long socks and

black polished shoes. We had caning and prefects and assembly on the asphalt.

'No,' I said.

'No playground at your private school?'

'No.'

'Lucky us.'

In January, the week of Beck's birthday—a week without snow, and warm—Frank and Beck were under the basketball hoop.

'There she is.' Frank turned toward me.

'Hi,' I said.

'Nice shirt.'

It was blue and white in checks.

'Thank you.'

'Why don't you two come for a drive?'

'Now?'

'Sure.'

Frank walked ahead of us and Beck rubbed his face and then his head with both hands, the way you rub a dog's head. Frank opened the car door for me.

Inside, the car was cream leather with a tint of rose. Beck sat in the backseat and didn't smile at all, not even when Frank put on 'Ain't No Use in Crying.' I put one of my hands behind me, between the seats for him to take, but he just ignored it. Finally, he gave in, leaning forward and wrapping his arms around my chest, over my black coat and blue shirt, kissing the side of my head.

Frank was from Queens, he explained, but he didn't set foot there now—except at the airport. He had offices at JFK and LaGuardia and Newark. He drove the way he walked, in a glide or as if on water, all the way down Lexington and over to Broadway, the leather on the steering wheel whirring beneath his palm.

Tribeca was all old buildings, gray and in blocks. There were hardly any trees. 'Drop the car at the garage?' Frank said, handing Beck the keys.

'I'll go with you,' I said.

'Don't be silly,' Frank said. 'It's cold. He'll only be a minute.'

* * *

The lobby was terra cotta and slate. The doorman wore a black suit. His hair was long for a doorman. In the elevator, all black with cherry wood, Frank held onto a metal handrail. The floor numbers clicked by in red letters like my alarm clock. Frank was on 9. When he opened the door, the wood on the floor was the color of a rare pear. The living room was at the far end, down a wooden step to two black leather couches. In the corner was an urn with the branches of a cherry blossom tree.

'Make yourself at home,' Frank said. He acted so casual. The kitchen was black and polished. On a counter was a blender and a box of instant protein packs. On the fridge were two photographs. One was of an office, three women standing about with champagne glasses as if at a party. The other was of a woman on a beach, her hair short and wet and dark.

'My sister,' Frank said.

'Where does she live?'

'Maui.'

'What's her name?'

'Elise.'

The walls were largely windows, on three sides. I could see New York Harbor and Chinatown and the Hudson River.

'Walk around,' Frank told me. I went clockwise, trailing my hand on the cold windowpanes, looking out at the sheer drop.

'Is that a French name?' I asked.

He was looking at his mail. 'My parents were French.'

'Frank isn't French.'

'It's not my real name.' He was throwing most of the mail in the trash.

'What's your real name?'

'François.'

'You didn't like it?'

He laughed. 'Not in Queens, no.' He dropped a few letters into a drawer, then snapped the drawer shut.

'You walk well,' he said.

'Do I?' I liked a compliment. It helped me know where I stood.

'Definitely.'

Outside, the bare trees were brittle, the buildings gleamed. Above the Hudson River, the sun was darkening. The blinds were the same cherry wood as in the elevator. Frank went to the fridge and opened it so I saw beer in brown bottles, sticks of individually wrapped mozzarella cheese. He twisted off a beer bottle cap. I played with the blinds; when they moved, they bent like reeds.

The intercom rang.

'Shall we answer it?' Frank asked, sipping from his bottle.

'Of course.'

His beautiful eyes looked dark. Beads of water had formed on his brown beer bottle.

'It's Beck,' I said.

'All right.' He left his bottle on the counter, moving to the intercom. 'You're sure now?'

My voice went hard. 'Yes.'

'Okay, darling,' he said.

On the Hudson, a sailboat motored upstream. 'Pretty, isn't it?' Frank asked, coming up behind me. He put his hands on my shoulders, still holding his bottle of beer. I felt my hair rise, as with static.

Then Beck came in the front door, cheeks stained with cold. 'Hey,' he said, so Frank turned from me; Beck came to us and dropped his car keys in Frank's hand. 'What's going on?'

'Looking at the view,' Frank said, slipping his keys into his pants pocket.

'Nice, huh?'

'Why don't you show her around?' Frank said.

In the hallway, behind the kitchen, I raised my arms to put them around Beck's neck. I was so glad he was there.

'Betsy,' he said, his cheek cold, the wool of his peacoat rough. He took down my hands, laughing. 'Don't.'

'Why not?'

'Frank.'

'What about Frank?'

'I don't know. You know. I just—I work for him.'

The towels in the bathroom were thick and fresh and white. At the edge of the Jacuzzi was a blue glass ashtray. Frank's bedroom was all green, except for the curtains, which had panels of white lace.

'What do you think?' Frank asked, back in the kitchen. He was sitting in one of the high chairs, his right ankle crossed on his knee. The sun had almost set, its light amber and soft with dust.

'It's lovely.'

A helicopter passed between the Twin Towers.

'Well, that's good, isn't it, Beck?' Frank asked. 'I always like to impress a girl like Betsy.'

'Frank impresses all the girls,' Beck said, so Frank smirked, holding onto his ankle in his ribbed trouser sock.

They walked back to Frank's room and I took a cup of water from a water cooler in the kitchen. I sat on the leather couch in the lounge. On the glass coffee table was a glass figurine in the shape of naked woman with raised knees. It was small and heavy, like a stone in the hand. I rubbed it on my sweater to get my fingerprints off. I picked up a magazine: *British Vogue*.

'You can take that if you like,' Frank told me.

'That's all right.'

'It's late,' Beck said.

'You want to go?' Frank asked. 'I'll take you.'

'Don't worry about it,' Beck said.

Frank took out his keys. 'I'll drive.'

He lit a cigarette just before we left. 'Jesus, man,' Beck said, when Frank took it on the elevator, so Frank laughed, making a gesture with his hand.

Outside, it was night. The avenues were lit. Frank's last name was Ravell, he told me. 'It's French. I like French things. You could be French.'

'No.'

'But you are not American. Your parents are—'

'English.'

'So we are European.'

'Beck's mother is from Iceland.'

'Where do you live, exactly?'

He was on 60th Street.

'64th Street.'

'Which number?'

'Just drop us on the corner,' Beck raised his voice.

'Hey,' Frank said, looking in the rearview mirror, 'where the fuck is Seth?'

Beck shrugged.

'Find him, would you?'

'You like him, don't you?' Beck asked me.

'Who? Frank? No.'

'You were all over him.'

'I was not.'

'All that European shit.'

'That was him.' We stood against the wall, under my stoop. It had grown colder, the wind gusting from the park and dry leaves scraping against the sidewalk. 'It's cold.'

He rearranged my scarf. 'You do like him.'

'Where did you meet him?'

'Through some guy, years ago.'

'What do you do for him, anyway? What does he do?'

'He's in trucking.'

'So you load trucks for him?'

'Things like that.'

There was a card in my coat pocket. It had smooth raised letters. I went to pull it out. Then I realized what it was. I should have given it to Beck, right then. But I didn't. 'It's freezing,' I said, wiping a strand of hair from my mouth.

'Go on.' He pushed at me, pulled me back to kiss him. 'Get inside.'

The house smelled of roast lamb and potatoes and squash. My mother was on the kitchen telephone. The lights were yellow and red. The television was on C-Span in the living room. On the stairs, I pulled the card from my pocket. *"Frank Ravell,"* it said, *"66 Leonard,"* with three telephone numbers. The cell phone number had been circled.

'What are you looking at?' my father asked. He was right below me, before the dining table. He had his hands in his trouser pockets.

'Nothing.'

'It's late. Where have you been?'

'I was with Beck.'

'Where with Beck?'

'In the park—and then a coffee shop.'

'You should get in before dark.'

'I'm sorry.' I put the card in my pocket.

'Let me see that.'

'Dad.'

'Let me see it.'

'It's just a card.'

I handed it across the banister to him. 'Whose is this?'

'It's Beck's. He works for him.'

'Why do you have his card?'

'So I can reach Beck. That's what he said.'

'What's what who said?'

'Beck.'

My father handed back the card. He shrugged and waved his hand. 'Anyway, it's dinnertime.'

Eric was a better student than I was. Every night, he went from dinner to his room, closing the door to study. He liked Noam Chomsky and Thomas Pynchon. He had a poster of Philip Glass. He liked talking about these things—about authors and musicians—more than about other things. Once, Sylvia asked me what Eric thought of Beck, but I didn't know what he thought. He had seen him at school, but we had never mentioned him, either of us.

I put Frank's card in my wallet, underneath my bus pass. 'Why keep that?' Sylvia wanted to know.

'I don't know. Just in case.'

'You didn't seem to like him too much.'

'I know.'

'So throw it out.'

* * *

Beck picked me up from school and we went to the playground, and Tommy was talking to Sharon and her friend Didi from Wagner High School. I kept looking around, half afraid Frank would show up and half wanting him to.

I sat on Beck's lap on the bench and his coat smelled damp but his skin was warm and he sang 'She's the One': *'Oh she can take you but if she wants to break you she's gonna find that ain't so easy to do.'*

Then it snowed, three times in one week. Beck and Tommy and I were in a coffee shop on 85th Street and Lexington, in a blue vinyl booth beside the window. Tommy kept adding sugar to his coffee, pouring it higher and higher on his spoon until Beck said, 'Quit it.' Then Frank pulled up on Lexington in a shiny black four-wheel-drive. He got out of the car and stood on the sidewalk in a camel-hair coat. Wind blew the snow around and Beck went out to meet him. I watched him scraping the sidewalk with his sneaker, the way he did when he was nervous. Finally, Frank got back in the car, the exhaust still running, and Beck came in to get me.

'What is it?' I asked.

I spilled my hot chocolate getting up. It was the color of dried lilac.

'Frank wants us to go downtown.'

'Now?'

'He wants me to pick up something first. Then I'll meet you.'

'You want me to go with Frank?'

He glared at me, like I should keep my voice down, like maybe I was embarrassing him. 'No big deal,' he said, putting his hand on my back, pushing me ahead of him out the door.

The snowflakes turned to water on my black down jacket. Beck opened the back door of Frank's car. 'Get in.'

'Hi, honey,' Frank said, turning down his techno music.

'I'll see you soon,' Beck softened up suddenly.

'Close the fucking door,' Frank said. 'It's freezing.'

He lit a cigarette, cracking the top of his window so the smoke curled out. He drove around the corner, down Park Avenue, which was all white. A patch of snow slid down a green awning.

'Why can't Beck come?'

''Cause he's doing something. He'll meet up with us.'

I hoped no one saw me. I hoped my mother didn't, or my father. Frank flicked his cigarette stub out the window, red embers hitting the windowpane. 'So, how are you, sweetie?' he asked.

'All right.'

'Nervous?'

'No.'

It was like when your friend leaves you alone with their parents and you have to talk to them. Only more than that. We stopped at a light on 42nd Street, everyone crowded on the curb with their foldable umbrellas and their rubber shoes. 'Why don't you hop out, honey, get in the front seat?'

Outside, the snow listed about. Water had risen in the gutters. I felt the cold inside my boots and something went through me— like fear, or the beginning of crying. I let out a sound but no one looked at me.

'You have snow on your hair,' Frank said. 'It looks pretty.'

'Thank you.'

'I'd touch it, but I'd just get wet.'

Back on Lexington, snow rose on newspaper stands and bicycle seats and on metal garbage cans. Frank played Sade on his stereo. It was one of my favorite songs: 'Haunt Me.'

'I had a daughter like you once myself, Betsy. But she died.'

'That's terrible.'

'Greatest tragedy of my life.'

'How old was she?'

'Six.'

For a moment, I thought I'd get out of the car. I put my hand on the door handle. If I did get out, I thought, I would just have to wonder. I would go around all the time wondering what Frank wanted, what could happen with him. The window was cool on my forehead.

'I'm sorry,' I said.

'Thank you.'

'What did she die of?'

'Cancer.'

Snow piled up on ledges and branches. It fell into dumpsters and garbage cans and doorways.

'Where are we going?'

'Tribeca.'

A valet took the car. He was black and had a black sweatshirt with red lining in the hood. Frank took my hand as we crossed the street. 'You need to lighten up.'

'I'm sorry.'

We walked from Church Street to Leonard, snow turning to slush and running water.

His doorman was drinking cappuccino, foam on his upper lip. Inside the elevator, snow melted on Frank's coat. Beads of water shone on his black sweater.

'Shoes off.'

He leaned down in the hallway and pulled off my boots. He smelled of something bitter, licorice or anisette. 'Your socks—'

My feet looked pale, almost yellow.

'I'll put them in the dryer. They'll be ready in five minutes.'

From his room, I heard the glide of a wooden drawer. He tossed socks down the hall, black and soft. Then I heard the dryer.

'Sit down,' he said, going to the kitchen, motioning to his couches. 'Do you drink wine?'

'Sometimes.'

I picked up the glass figurine, then put it back.

'That is not a naked woman.'

He took a bottle from a rack above the fridge, uncorking it on the slate kitchen console.

'What is it?'

'Well, it is when it's lying down, but if you put her on her knees, she's a woman praying.'

I laughed. My laughter seemed odd in his great bare space.

'Here—' When he moved in his black trouser socks, he made no noise at all. 'Your glass.'

'Thank you.'

'You'd better clean that off with your sweater.'

It felt like a sparrow, rounded and smooth.

He took a big sip of his wine. 'You look good on my couch.'

'Do I?'

'Yes. I thought you would.' I set the figurine on her knees. He looked at it and laughed. He wasn't thinking about it.

'How are those socks?'

'Nice.'

He was like a man who looks at you in the street, a man you would never speak to usually, but who attracts you somehow—the way he smiles or moves or talks to you as if he already knows you—so when you look away you feel guilty, a little sick and aroused and disturbed. He sat beside me on the couch.

'What's a girl like you doing with Beck?'

'I like Beck.'

'You can do better.' His nails were square and manicured. He looked at my pants. 'You sure like corduroys, don't you?'

'Yes.'

'You should wear skirts.'

'That's what Beck says.'

'Does he?'

'Yes.'

'You shouldn't hang out in Queens.'

'Why not?'

'First, because you're too good for Queens. And second, because I own that dump.'

'I thought Beck's dad owned it.'

'There is no Beck's dad.'

'Yes there is.'

'Yeah, they met in court, when Beck was nine. He looked at the kid and said, *"He's not my son."* Nice dad.'

'I thought the tests said he was.'

'They did.'

'How could he say that, then?'

'The kid's a bastard—not that that means much now.' He got up. 'Talking about Beck, I should check my machine.'

He took off his sweater. Underneath, he was wearing a white T-shirt. I could see his shoulder blades, long and bony. He cradled the phone on his shoulder, folding his sweater on the countertop.

'May I use the bathroom?'

'Go ahead.'

Again, the towels were fresh and thick and white. The mirror at the sink was lit with round bulbs. I liked my corduroys.

'You all right there?'

'Yes.'

He was leaning against the counter, drinking his wine. The scar above his jaw was shining.

'Beck got held up.'

'He did?' I took a breath. I wasn't surprised at all. I would have been surprised if Beck had shown up, if everything had been all right.

'I should go.'

He held out my glass to me. 'Finish your wine.'

'No, really.'

'Go on.' What was Beck doing? On the coffee table was the *New York Times*, unopened. 'I won't hurt you.'

'No—'

'I like looking at you. I admit that. But there's nothing wrong with that, is there?'

'No.'

'Do you like looking at me?'

He wasn't handsome exactly. His hair was almost unnaturally dark, his mouth not thin yet not beautiful, his skin marked from the sun. Still, he bristled with something—not anger but force, some kind of need.

'It's all right,' he laughed. 'You don't have to say.'

The wine was dark and heavy. I sat on one couch and he on the other.

'I guess I do,' I said. He spread his arms out. 'I mean, I notice you.'

'Do you?'

'Sometimes. At the playground.' I looked at my glass.

'The thing about you, Betsy—'

'Yes?'

He smiled, a small knowing smile. 'You have this purity.'

'No, I don't.'

'Yet at the same time, you're very sexy.'

I set my glass on the coffee table. I walked over to the window on the Hudson River. The water was icy. The docks were full of snow.

'*Old Stewball was a racehorse, and I wish he were mine. He never drank water, he always drank wine.* You know that song?'

'No.'

'It was the name of our boat, in Antigua. We used to tie up at the docks and the boys on shore would sing it.'

'To you?' He went to the kitchen and poured himself more wine.

'They were all fishermen's sons. They'd get salt streaks all along their arms.'

'What made you think of them?'

'I don't know.'

'I wish you'd look at me instead of out the window.'

I turned around. 'I'm sorry.'

'Come here.'

I stepped back toward the kitchen. He set down his glass and stepped over to me. He lifted me up, by the waist, onto the kitchen console.

'How old are you, Betsy?'

'Sixteen.'

I didn't like his mouth. He had nice eyelashes, though, long and dark.

'How old are you?'

'Forty-one.'

He leaned so close to me, grazing my cheekbone with his, his mouth so close I thought he was going to kiss me. I held his shoulders, steadying myself, pulling away.

'You need someone older.' He was tucking my hair behind my ear. 'You're not an easy girl, are you?'

His hands were on either side of me then, pressed down on the black console so the muscles in his arms tightened. All this energy came to me, like heat or anger—or just the truth of what he wanted. When he kissed me, it was almost a relief, as if the wave I had seen building finally fell. He pulled me to the edge of the console. He moved his hand down my stomach and I moved my hips, ever so slightly, to make it easier.

'Lie down with me.'

'No.'

'Just for a minute.'

He was pressing against me. Then he picked me up and I laughed. Laughing made it seem less real. So did the wine. He carried me back to his bed and lay me down. His room was so quiet. I heard the mantel clock ticking. The light fell in pieces through the curtain. Then I closed my eyes, the way I did with Ray, the better to feel him—and to ignore who he was. Frank moved my hand to his penis, but that was too much.

'I'm sorry,' I said, moving from underneath him.

'It's all right.'

'I have to go.'

He pulled me over to him. He moved his tongue into my mouth. It was hard to stop. It was hard when I felt his hands, so smooth and firm on my legs.

'Please,' I said.

He lay back and fixed his pants and stared at the ceiling. 'You're not a tease are you, Betsy?'

'No.'

'No one likes a tease.' He turned his head and lay his eyes on me. 'Don't worry,' he said. 'I can wait.'

Then I didn't see him. It was Valentine's Day and Beck showed up at school with a rose. His mother was at home, sick, so we went to the boat pond where we had gone months ago, the day Raymond had left. Now everything was icy but Beck's mouth and his breath. He blew on my hands, and rubbed them between his, so I moved them under his peacoat and his sweater and T-shirt onto his chest, which was warm and smooth.

'You're so sweet,' he said.

'I am not.'

'You are.'

He was so sure. My stomach felt queasy, me with my chin on his shoulder, looking at the white pond. I hoped I never saw Frank again. If I did, I had decided, I wouldn't speak to him. I wouldn't speak to him or touch him again ever.

In Queens, Frank let himself in the front door. 'Hi, beautiful.' I wasn't speaking to him. I got up from the couch and Beck did as well, rubbing his head the way he had taken to doing, half yawning, and then straightening up. Seth and Tommy lit cigarettes.

'There's something in the car,' Frank motioned, so Beck went out the front door and this flush went through me, like it did in airports sometimes, when it was too hot and I had to sit down. I went to the bathroom and one of the ceiling bulbs was out. The sliding mirrors were dark and speckled. On the sink was a blue disposable razor.

'Betsy.' Frank rattled the loose metal doorknob.

Just like when my father spoke sharply to me, or when the headmaster in grade school called us to attention, I straightened up. I opened the door and Frank closed it behind him. 'Are you all right?'

I wasn't saying anything.

'What is it?' He took my face in his hands. 'You don't look so good.'

I heard television from the living room. I could smell leather and milky skin lotion.

'Where's Beck?' I asked.

'He'll be back.' He moved my hair behind my ear the way he had at his loft. 'Don't brush me off,' he said. 'I don't deserve that.'

'I'm sorry.'

Already, I was talking to him.

'Darling.'

His voice was so dark and smooth. It was like night, a flower that opens in the dark.

His thumb was on the button of my corduroys. He slipped the button through, then moved his hand down. Once he had touched me, naked, inside, I didn't try anymore. I lay back on the white tiles and he used his tongue on me. Dust drifted like tumbleweed under the door and he made me come. I knew it was coming, for the first time ever, because he told me so.

Afterwards, in the living room, I couldn't look at him. He raised his hand at the door, waving goodbye to us all. He shouldn't have left me there, I thought. What if Beck had guessed? What if he found out? He was staring at me, arms crossed on his white T-shirt, legs spread on the scuffed floor.

'What the fuck was that?' he asked.

'What?'

'Frank—in the bathroom with you.'

'He came in.'

'What for?'

'He said you were using the car.'

'Fucking A.'

'What did Frank have in the car?' I asked.

'You know why I wouldn't tell you that?'

'Why?'

''Cause I care about you.'

I was scared he would kiss me, Frank still in my mouth.

'Can we leave?' I asked.

I felt sick then, sick and afraid at how I was. I spent most of the day sick, so Sylvia frowned at me over chicken à la king in the cafeteria, so Henry asked what was wrong. I couldn't say, though. If I said, they would all tell me, *'Stay away from Frank,'* as if I didn't know that, as if it were easy.

At night, I lay in bed and the light from the streetlamp made a line across the floor—across the hallway to Raymond's door, which was shut.

I remembered the white tiles and the smell of leather and of dust and I wished Frank were there right then. I wished he were outside in a car waiting for me.

Beck came to school and I told him I was sick and that the next week I had exams. I went to the pay phone by school and stood there, wanting to call Frank. At night, I took the telephone into my room and held his card in my hand, and once I did call but he wasn't there.

Then one day I came out of school and they were both there: Frank in his black four-wheel-drive with the front window down, Beck crossing the street to me. 'Come on,' he said, nodding to the car, and I shook my head. 'What's wrong?'

'I have to study.'

'Now?'

He took hold of my elbow. Frank tossed his cigarette out the window.

'I have a test.'

Frank closed his window and started the ignition. Miss Porter came over. 'Are you all right, Betsy?'

'I'm fine.'

Beck turned up his palms, like he didn't understand, walking backwards to the car. 'You sure?' he asked.

'I can't. I'm sorry.'

'Do you know those people, Betsy?'

'Yes.'

'Did someone say something to upset you?'

'No.'

We watched them drive off.

'What a massive car,' Miss Porter said.

Every morning, I woke at seven-thirty. I left the house at eight a.m., stopping for a coffee to go at Eat Here Now. One day I stepped out the door and the sky was the clear clean blue of the blue inside a flame and Frank's car was there, across the street, and my heart slammed as his car door did when he got out.

'Betsy,' he said, and I looked back at the house. My parents were inside. 'Get in the car.'

'No.'

He took my forearm.

'Just get in.'

I turned my head from the house, as if my parents might be watching.

'Oh, relax,' he said once we had reached Park Avenue. It was warm in the car. On the floor was a bag from Starbucks. 'Have one. Have a hot chocolate. All the girls in France drink hot chocolate.'

I had been to France.

'What's going on with you?'

'Nothing.'

'You hurt my feelings the other day.'

'I did?'

'Ignoring me when I came to your school.'

'I'm sorry.'

'We had a few moments, Betsy. That's all. It's nothing to be scared about.'

The trees were bare on Park Avenue. I saw a man in a fool's hat, purple and made of fleece.

'It's not that I don't like you,' Frank said. 'I do like you, very much. But I told you, I can wait.'

He glanced at me, eyes heavy as if from sleep or thought, his skin smooth with lotion and his slight scar raised. We stopped at a light and his eyes fell on me with a sort of quiet fullness. He was still, suddenly. He was satisfied. He was not the man in the playground, striding across the pavement for Beck or for Seth, not the man on Mott Street with his legs up on the coffee table. I smiled at him.

'You mean that?' I asked.

'Sure I do.'

'Really?'

'Really.'

Maybe he did. 'That's nice,' I said.

'I'm nice.'

Maybe he was. Maybe I shouldn't be so afraid. Maybe I was afraid not so much of Frank, but of Beck finding out.

On 90th Street, before we reached my school, he stopped the car.

'It is good hot chocolate,' I said.

'I thought you'd like it.'

'Thanks for driving me.'

'You're welcome.' He turned off the radio.

'I like Beck so much.'

He looked straight ahead, drinking his coffee. 'I know you do. But you'll outgrow him.'

'No, I won't.'

'You already have.' He turned his face to me. 'That's why you're talking to me.'

'No, it's not.'

He wrapped my hair in his fingers, letting it fall and lifting it again. 'Then why are you talking to me?'

'You picked me up at my house.'

'It's a two-way street, Betsy.'

I felt bad then. I put my hand on the door handle.

'I'm sorry,' he said. 'I want you to realize for yourself.'

'Realize what?'

'How attracted we are to each other.'

I was attracted to him: to the wheel whirring beneath his palm, to his body with all this energy, to his face hard one minute and open the next.

'You're not a little girl.'

'No.'

'Sometimes I think you act that way so you don't have to make your own decisions.'

I made decisions—I just didn't keep them.

'Don't look that way,' Frank said. 'I think you're more grown up than you let on.'

Maybe I was.

'You're playing with Beck.'

'That's not true.'

Beck thought I was so pure, so untouched. He didn't know me at all—though that was partly why I liked him, liked the way he saw me, the way he adored me.

When Frank kissed me, he tasted of coffee and foam. He moved his tongue deep into my mouth and it was impossible, I thought. It would be impossible not to sleep with him.

Beck asked what we did at Houghton for fun, and I told him we did the usual things: went to movies and parties and plays at school.

'Plays,' he laughed. 'We don't do plays.'

'What do you do?'

'You've seen.'

'Go to Queens?'

'Queens. Brooklyn. Sometimes the island.'

'Do Seth and Tommy work for Frank?'

'Yeah.'

'Where did you meet him?'

'He likes you.'

'Who does?'

'Frank—he likes girls.'

'That means he likes me?'

'He wanted to meet you. He saw you with me, in the playground. He told me to bring you around.'

'When?'

'Months ago. Don't worry. He likes lots of girls.'

Like I said, some things happen all around you and they happen fast. Frank came to the playground and I pretended to ignore him and he pretended back. I could feel him, though. I could feel him the way I used to feel Ray, waiting and watching, sidling along the walls of the house.

Beck and I went to the playground and his house. Sylvia and I watched cable and drank Cokes and smoked clove cigarettes. Then one day I met my mother at the Whitney. It was about four p.m. and just getting dark. We walked up Madison Avenue to a little store that sold linen. My mother's hair was in a long blond braid, her scarf red and her boots shiny black. The stores and the galleries were still open and bright. Then I saw Frank in his silver Mercedes driving beside us. He had his right window down and was looking out at us. Maybe he didn't see my mother or maybe he didn't realize she was my mother. Either way, my face turned white.

'Do you know that man?' my mother asked, sharply.

'No.'

Just as I had imagined, she didn't like him at all. She took my arm and pulled me close to the buildings.

'He seems to know you,' she said, as they looked at each other, neither of them smiling.

The next day, on Lexington after school, I stopped at a pay phone. The wind was blowing people's scarves around. '*Jesus Saves*' had been scratched onto the telephone.

I dialed Frank's cell phone number. 'Yeah,' he said, like he was being bothered.

'Frank?'

'Yeah.'

'It's Betsy.'

'Betsy.' He paused. 'Where are you?'

'85th Street.'

'What are you doing?'

'Nothing.'

I could hear some kind of techno music on his stereo. 'Give me ten minutes.'

There wasn't any snow, but it was still cold. A woman stopped and fixed the barrette in her hair. Two boys went by with fencing equipment. What if someone went looking for me—Sylvia or Henry or my parents? What if they couldn't find me?

'So where will it be?' Frank asked, picking me up at the curb. 'Queens?' He laughed, clipping his cell phone to his belt.

'You scared me.'

'When?'

'Yesterday. That was my mother.'

'Attractive woman.'

'She asked me about you, if I knew you.'

'What did you say?'

'I said no.'

'No harm done, then.'

'She was suspicious. I thought she might tell my father.'

He laughed. 'All right. I'm sorry. I couldn't resist. It was only a few blocks.'

'You followed us?'

He turned the music up. 'It was nothing.'

'Frank.'

'Come on, I'll make it up to you.'

He took my hand in the street. He held it firmly, walking me the way a man walks a child, thinking of something else. Upstairs, dusk gave the wood floor a pinkish sheen. Frank turned my back to the river. 'Christ,' he said.

'What is it?'

'Christ. *Christ* is the most beautiful word in the English language. Say it.'

'Christ.'

'That's how beautiful you are.'

'I am not.'

He laughed. He took off his jacket. 'I'm glad you called.'

'Are you?'

He took off his sweater. 'Come here,' he said.

His sheets had no scent. They were ivory, the color of parchment paper, with crimson flowers. He kissed me like he owned me, the way I knew he would.

Then he was taking off my shirt. 'Have you thought about me?'

'Yes.' My stomach felt bad. I had to get up suddenly. 'I'm sorry,' I said and went to the bathroom.

'You're nervous.' He took my cold hands when I came back. He pulled me to him, stroking my hair. I could feel my heart in my chest, rapid as a bird's. 'Betsy, Betsy,' he said, kissing me hard suddenly, and then I was helping him with my corduroys, helping him with my underpants.

The hair on his chest was thick and half gray. He was thinner than Beck, wiry and lean. He moved straight into me, kissing me too hard. I held onto his arms, wanting him to stop. He didn't, though, and I said nothing. There was no going back once a man was inside you.

Finally, he came, his hands on the headboard.

I started to cry.

'Don't,' he said, getting off me, going to the bathroom.

'Why not?'

He came back with a washcloth, rubbing me clean.

''Cause I can hear you.'

* * *

Later, in the kitchen drinking seltzer water, he watched me, leaning back against the sink. 'It'll get better,' he said. He had his pants back on and a fresh white T-shirt. 'I'm going to take you out. Would you like that?'

He didn't get it. He didn't get it at all. I wasn't going to see him again. I wasn't going to talk to him, ever. My finger was cold and wet, drawing a *B* on his windowpane for *Beck, Betsy*.

'Can you get away? For a night?'

'Maybe.'

After France, after Raymond and Eric had their picture taken at L'Hotel Oiseau, after Brussels and Luxembourg and the ferry to England, Raymond went back to Antigua with packets of heroin sewn into his jacket. They found it at the airport and for a moment, because my father was behind Raymond in line, because he saw what was happening, my father hung back. It was the surprise, he said later, the need for a moment to prepare, to plan a defense. Raymond claimed Dad would have climbed back onto the plane if he could have, gone out the back door, if there were one. Still, it was my father who went with Raymond to the police station. It was my father's name that appeared first in the Antigua newspapers. Raymond's picture was grainy and indistinct. My father's was a government headshot that had appeared in the paper many times before: a picture showing his intelligence and gravity, his lean features and smooth forehead. There was also a photograph of my mother and Eric and Raymond and me taken the summer before at the pool. My mother's honeysuckle hair was shorter than usual, just to the shoulders, and her legs were in the water, feet extended so the tips of her toes showed, and her eyes were made up, even poolside, to be deep and almost sorrowful. *'Happier times for Mrs. Scott,'* said the caption. *'Raymond, 18, Betsy, 12, Eric, 11.'*

Frank put me in a cab. I felt bad, and also afraid. What if Beck found out?

Beck picked me up from school the next day and all the blood went out of my face when I saw him. 'What's wrong?' he asked, and it was awful, the way he backed away a little.

'Nothing.'

It was windy and clear. We walked around the corner, stopping beside a stoop. 'What is it?' he asked, me in the corner and him in front of me, his hand against the wall. The wind rattled a can in the gutter and I started to cry.

'Betsy, are you sick? What is it?'

'I'm fine,' I said, and then I saw it light into him: the truth. I saw it cross his face.

'No, don't fucking tell me, 'cause I know.' He didn't even raise his voice, but it was as if he did. I wanted to put my arms around him. 'And you know what? You know what?' He raised his hands in the air. 'I'm not even going to go there. Not now. I'll see you later.'

I walked home by myself, shivery as if from the cold, but it wasn't the cold. The whole time I was walking, I was thinking maybe Frank would show up, in his car beside me. When I got home, I went up to my room, and at dinner I hardly ate, so my mother asked if I was sick and I said no. Then I called Beck at his house but his mother answered. She had an accent. It sounded German. She told me Beck wasn't home and wouldn't be until late.

I knew Beck wouldn't come to school to break up with me, so when I saw him the next day, relief came over me in a hot wave. 'Come here,' he said, his face all closed and impassive, the way it usually was, I guess, the way Sylvia and Henry complained about.

We went back around the corner, to the same stoop, and I said, 'I'm sorry,' covering my face with my hands and crying again so Beck said, 'Jesus, Jesus, Betsy. Stop it.'

'I didn't mean to. I don't even—'

'Stop it.' He took my wrist. 'I mean it.' People were walking by, looking at us, so I turned my face. Beck moved in closer and lowered his voice. 'I know what's going on. But I can't completely blame you. I kind of let it happen—not because I wanted to, but because that's the way it is.'

'The way *what* is?'

'The way it is with Frank.'

What did he mean, he *let it happen?* It would have happened with Frank or with someone else because that's the way I was.

'Can we go?' I asked. 'Can we not stand here?'

He shook his head. Maybe he was finished with me.

'Can we go to your house?' I asked.

'Now? I don't know about now, Betsy.' I rubbed my face and my head with my hands, the way he always did, so he said, 'Come on.'

Then, in his room, we lay on his bed and Beck looked up at the ceiling, hands on his chest. 'Of course, you have fucked it up. Between us.'

'I know.'

'You should go.'

'No.'

'Go on. Get out of here.'

'Beck.'

'Go on.'

I put on my clothes, starting to cry again. 'You shouldn't pick me up at school,' I said.

'I'll pick you up when I want to.'

Frank called the school. The message was taped to my locker. *'Frank. Four o' clock, Park Avenue.'* I told myself I wouldn't go. I told myself Beck would come instead, at three-thirty, and we would leave together. Beck didn't come, though, and Frank was already there, double-parked in his silver Mercedes. He was on his cell phone and closed it up when he saw me.

'Get in.' He turned on the ignition, looking at the rearview mirror as he pulled out. 'What's wrong?' he asked. 'You look stirred up.'

'Why do I like you?'

'You don't have to like me, Betsy.' His face was hard, yet

interesting to me. His cold blue eyes, Atlantic and deep. We took the FDR Drive all the way down the island. I had made Beck wait so long and then Frank just moved his hand inside my shirt and touched my breast, like he had a right to.

The sun in March was weak, like light at the beginning of day, its rays long and flat. Frank came on Fridays, waiting in his car on the corner. Maybe Beck knew about this and maybe he didn't. Maybe he was acting the way I had with Ray, letting things happen and then pretending I hadn't.

We walked downtown, and Beck wanted us to go to the playground, but I wouldn't. 'Why not?' he asked me, his eyes all sly.

'I don't know.'

'*I don't know,*' he mimicked.

I was tired of sitting on the bench watching him play ball. I was tired of Tommy winking at me as if he knew something. 'I should go,' I told Beck, and he nodded at me, hardly even holding my gaze, wiping his forehead with his T-shirt.

I sat on the cool edge of Frank's Jacuzzi turning over his blue glass ashtray. It was the blue of a hazy morning in Antigua, a blue washed through with cloud, blue of my uniform and the flower at the edge of the road, of my mother's eyes behind her sunglasses and Eric's in the late afternoon as we dragged through the white dust after school, dirt in our brown leather sandals, eating hard candies from the general store: mint and vanilla and butterscotch.

'Can I stay at Sylvia's tonight?' I asked when she picked up the phone. She never did suspect me. Sylvia had Frank's cell phone number, in case my mother looked for me, but she didn't. Frank and I went to dinner at Raoul's and Match and Express. He liked steak frites and filet mignon and mussels. He liked bistros: the lights dim yellow, the tables dark wood, the napkins cloth. Frank slipped his hand under the table to my knee. He didn't like to touch me in public. It was disrespectful, he said.

I was something delicate when I was with Frank. Everything around was in a quiet hush. He winked at me and he was like this gold light inside me, a secret burning thread.

* * *

Some nights, we ordered in: the same dishes from the same restaurants, which I slipped, as my mother would, onto china plates already warmed in the oven. Frank poured us wine, and when we were finished I cleared the table and Frank smoked a cigarette.

I was another person altogether with Frank. I was more serious, and not just because Frank was serious, but because Frank didn't think of me as a girl, he told me, but as a young woman. He told me this as if he was complimenting me, sitting with his legs up on his couch, smoking a cigar and regarding me as if I pleased him. I wasn't dumb, though.

'What difference does it make?' I asked, carrying the dishes to the sink.

'You're mature.'

'Do you think so?'

'You're flaky, of course. Anyone hanging out with Beck has to be flaky. You won't fall apart, though, if something bad happens.'

'You don't think I'm mature at all.'

He smiled.

'You're just telling me to be mature so I don't get you into trouble.'

'That's my girl.'

I watched him dressing one Saturday morning, looking at himself in the full-length mirrors inside his closet door. He had a meeting in Queens and put himself on the way most people put on outfits.

'What did you look like at my age?' I asked, sitting on the edge of his bed, waiting for him.

'Better,' he said, so we laughed.

'Would you have liked me?'

'Oh yes. I would have zeroed right in.'

'You think so?'

'I would have married you.'

'But not now.'

'Now you're too young.' He put on a metallic blue tie. 'And I'm fucked up.'

'Are you?'

'Of course.'

He liked French cuffs. He liked gold cuff links, or sometimes black.

'Maybe I'll marry Beck.'

He shook out his sleeve so the cuff link settled beneath his wrist bone. He lifted my chin in his hand, on his way to the kitchen. 'You will never marry Beck.'

I followed him to the kitchen, where he took a bag of ground coffee from the fridge, scooped some into his espresso maker. 'Were you married?'

'Sure, I was.'

'For how long?'

'Long enough.'

'You don't want to talk about it?'

'I'm not the kind that looks back.'

'I wish I could be like that.'

'Why can't you?'

'I just feel like it's there all the time—the past, things that happened.'

'What happened?'

'Things.'

He crossed his legs at the ankles. He looked so arrogant sometimes. 'Something happened,' he said, draining his cup, putting it behind him in the sink. 'Or you wouldn't be with me.'

I smiled. That was why I liked him. I liked him the first moment, because he saw me for who I was, he saw I had been through something. And it was something that would serve him. He wanted me for that. I was so glad for this. That he valued this. It made my eyes tingle as if I was going to cry. Around his pale blue iris was a dark blue circle.

'Don't cry about it, though.' He put his hand on my neck. 'Go on. Keep going.'

I wanted to tell him what it was. I wanted to tell him right then. I turned to him, but his face had closed. He had this slight smile on his lips, distant now, his hand pushing me away. 'Go on.'

* * *

Beck raised his chin when he saw me. He was leaning against a car outside school, acknowledging me but just barely. I didn't know why he picked me up if he was going to act that way.

'Are you all right?' I asked, and he rolled his eyes. He was so cold. He should have been cold, though, because of what I was doing. I wanted to apologize, but how could I, if I was going to see Frank again?

We walked to Central Park and kicked around the dirty snow and he said, 'Don't think I don't care, 'cause I do. I care about everything, every tiny fucking little thing with you, but you know, I can't deal.'

We were on a bench at the boat pond and he pulled me onto his lap. He never wore a hat or gloves or even a scarf, so I tried to warm him up, moving my hands in my leather gloves on his arms in his peacoat, and then I held onto him like something terrible was happening to us, when it was just me, really, me and what I was doing with Frank. We went home to Beck's, and maybe Beck wasn't saying how angry he was at me, but I could feel it, the way he pinned my wrists to the sheets in his bed, the way he moved hard into me. I got tears in my eyes and I hated him. Then a moment later I felt bad for him, as if I loved him, as if I wanted to stay with him always.

'Beck.' I put my arm across his chest.

'What?'

'Don't be mad.'

His muscles stiffened as if he was going to get up. He ran his fingers along my leg. I kissed his shoulder and he tasted of salt, and he was the one that cared about me; he was the one that would do anything for me and with me and because of me. *I will not see Frank again*, I told myself.

Then I went to school and I got a phone message from Frank again.

'4 o'clock, Park Avenue,' and I pictured his great empty blue eyes and the way he gazed at me, half pleased and half amused, so it made me sick at myself and disgusted.

* * *

Frank examined his face in the bathroom mirror: his long lashes, round eyes, taut skin. 'I look old,' he said.

He had lines beside his mouth. He had a crease on his high forehead. His chest hair was turning gray, from the divorce, he said, the death of his daughter.

He made popcorn and opened bottles of mineral water. He smoked brown cigarettes called Nat Shermans. 'Better than Queens?' he asked me.

'I'm not from Queens.'

He watched stupid movies, the kind of movies I would never watch usually.

'You hang out there.'

'Why don't you watch anything serious?'

'Why should I?'

'You're smart.'

'I see serious stuff all day.'

'Do you?'

'What do you think? I see things you couldn't imagine.'

'Bad things?'

He smiled, draining his mineral water. 'You're not such a saint yourself. Not even seventeen and fucking over your boyfriend.'

'Don't say that.'

He laughed. 'It's true.'

I didn't know what to say when people were mean that way. I could be mean, too, but not that bad. Raymond had been the meanest.

I went to his bedroom and lay on my back on the bed. I kept thinking he would get up and come in to see me. He didn't, though. He had lived in the loft for a year, but it still smelled new. The walls and the carpet and the bed smelled new. Even the pillows and the sheets smelled new. They smelled of fabric right from the store, not even washed. The floor smelled of wood and plastic. I should have been at home. I should have been with Beck or with Sylvia. I got tears in my eyes, not from sadness but from frustration, the way I wanted so much to leave, kept urging myself to leave, but just didn't do it, just didn't, ever, do it.

* * *

When I woke, the sky was empty gray and vague, a four a.m. sky, the clouds like sheets hung out to dry. The television was off and Frank was on the bed, naked but for his cotton pajama pants. 'Get up,' he said. His voice was cold. He took me to the bathroom and ran the shower. 'Wash,' he said, so I did. Then he held out a towel. He kissed my mouth.

He held my jaw between his fingers, which smelled of smoke. From the bed, the sky outside the windows moved from gray to white, not the faint misty cloud slipping down the rivers to the sea, but white the color of smoke and as dense, pressing at the windows with a kind of glare. It was easy for him to hurt me. Easy because he was strong. Easy because I would not let on that he was hurting me. Maybe, I even thought, I wanted him to hurt me—because if he hurt me, really hurt me, I might leave.

Beck walked without speaking, grasping my hand. 'He acts like he's French or something,' he said, drinking from his can of orange soda. 'But I've seen his house. I've seen where he grew up.'

'In Queens?' I asked.

'Yeah. Fucking garden gnomes and shit. Real impressive.'

In his bed, I cupped myself with my hand, my flesh sore and swollen.

'What is it?' Beck asked and I shook my head.

Frank gave me jelly, clear and cool so it didn't hurt after that. Grass appeared in the pavement cracks and the sun shone sleek on the tops of cars. Frank and I went to West Broadway, art in the windows and bright fantastic clothes. He bought me a crimson dress, long and smooth and cool, that he hung in a garment bag alongside his suits.

I watched, sitting on his bed. 'Do you go out with people your own age?'

'Of course.'

'Do you have photographs?'

'I don't keep photographs.'

'Here,' I said and handed him one of me.

'Where'd you get this?'

'From school.'

'What am I supposed to do with it?'

'I don't know.'

'Carry it in my wallet?'

I took it back from him. 'You don't have to be mean.'

For spring break, my family went to Bermuda. Our hotel was dark pink, the lawns green. Hibiscus trees flowered by the walls. Henry's mother sang there sometimes; her photograph was in the lobby. Dad didn't like resorts. He'd rather sail, he said, and the people were boring. I didn't see that the people at the Princess were so different from the people at Dad's club, but he did.

My mother didn't go out in the bright day sun, but came down to the beach in the late afternoons. She wore a straw hat and sunglasses and put her hair in a braid. She sat on a towel and watched Eric and me swim. Sometimes she swam also, and then it was for a long time, a long way out, her limbs pale under her bathing suit and the dark sea surface.

Eric was reading *Respect for Acting,* and I had brought *The Moviegoer,* which was Eric's favorite book. I got the darkest tan possible in six days, partly because I tan easily and partly because I thought Frank would like that. At night, we had piña coladas at a table looking over the sea. The air smelled of red bottle trees and dark patches moved on the water. In the sky, red light bled into violet and the sun was orange.

'It's quiet without Raymond,' my father said.

'It is,' my mother said.

Eric laughed, tipping back his chair. His hair looked bleached from the sun. I had no idea what he thought.

'A toast to Raymond,' my father said and we all moved forward, holding up our glasses.

Later, Eric and I read in our room. When I put down my book, he asked if I was finished and I said yes. With the lights out,

I could see the black night outside and Eric's shiny head on his pillow.

Our last night in Bermuda, my mother came into the bathroom. I was in the bathtub. The door was closed but not locked. 'Betsy.' She was in her nightgown, long and sheer.

'Yes.' I was using lavender bath salts, *The Moviegoer* on the bathmat.

'Is everything all right?'

'Yes.'

She rested against the sink counter. Her hair was down.

I covered my chest with bath bubbles.

'Nothing's going on, nothing you want to talk about?'

'No, I don't think so.'

'Nothing with Beck?'

'No.'

She rubbed one foot against the other, her toenail polish pale pink.

'Of course, you're allowed to have your private life. It's just I don't want you to feel you can't talk to me, or to your father.'

I turned on the hot tap. I didn't know what to say, so finally I said, 'Okay,' in this neutral voice because I didn't know what she wanted. She lifted an eyebrow brush from the counter, playing with the bristles.

'I was married at nineteen, you know. That's not so much older than you are now.'

'A little.'

'You're looking older, suddenly.'

'Am I?'

The mirror behind her was cloudy with steam. She looked at it and then back.

'Yes, I think you are. Not that it's bad. I just, you know, miss the little girl, too.'

'Of course she's right,' Frank said, lying on his ivory sheets with crimson flowers, his wall of window white with a sky full of snow. 'You *are* older.'

'But how can she tell?'

'She can tell the way I could tell that you had something going on.'

'You mean with Beck?'

'No. I mean something else.'

He got up from the bed. I saw him in the bathroom mirror, looking at his head left to right, checking himself.

'Do you want to know my secret?' I asked.

'Not really.' He ran his hand over his jaw.

'No?'

He lathered his face.

'Okay, a little bit.'

He was so uninterested. I opened the drawer beside the bed. There was a blank note card inside, *'66 Leonard'* engraved in blue on the bottom.

'You have nothing good to look at.'

'Oh, really?'

'No letters, no photographs.'

'I threw it all out. When my daughter died.'

'Where did your wife go?'

'My ex-wife.'

'Your ex-wife.'

'That's not my business anymore. That's why they call it "ex."'

'I'm sorry.'

He snapped the drawer shut. 'Anyway, don't snoop.' He tugged at the sheet. 'Get up. Take a shower.'

Sylvia came around the corner with me, her blond hair like a waterfall down her back. She was wearing black pants and high-heeled boots and a white long-sleeved T-shirt.

Frank had his hand on the gearshift. 'Darling,' he enthused. 'Get in. We'll take you home.'

She was meeting Henry.

'Is that your boyfriend?'

'Yes.'

'We should go to dinner, the four of us. What's your favorite restaurant?'

'Oh, I don't know,' Sylvia shrugged.

'Lutece? Raoul's?'

'Whatever.'

'We'll decide. I'll have Betsy tell you.'

'All right.'

She waved to me. Frank watched her walk down Park Avenue. 'Nice look,' he said.

'He's old,' Sylvia told me.

'Not really.'

'Someone should tell your parents.'

'You wouldn't.'

'No, but he's weird. He's like from this whole other world. So is Beck. No one knows what you're doing.'

'I'm not doing anything.'

'You're never around.'

I was glad not to be around. I didn't like Houghton. I didn't like the girls with their fancy clothes and the boys who made jokes about blowjobs. I didn't like Houghton parties, twenty of us in an apartment uptown, girls locking themselves in the bathroom, seniors getting drunk with their hair falling into their eyes.

'What did you mean that I was pure?' I asked Frank. He was squatting with his thin knees against the tub, the hair on his legs black and wet. He swirled the razor in the water.

'It's just a quality.'

'But I'm not, really.'

He was shaving the hair between my legs, carefully, infinitely slowly.

'Maybe not. But you seem it.'

He pressed a warm washcloth to me, then soaked it in the tub. 'Some people will value it. Other people will want to fuck it up.'

'What do you want?'

The water was white with soap.

'Tell me,' I said.

'What do you think?'

I thought it was both. I thought he both cared and didn't care, for reasons I would never know.

'I value you,' he finally said.

Cherry blossoms bloomed white in the park. Leaves came in on the maples and the oaks. We went to Raoul's on Prince Street, Henry in a blue button down, Sylvia in a tight black halter and pants, like her mother would have worn. Our waiter was Japanese, young with dyed yellow hair. 'Sir,' he kept saying, the way Beck did.

Henry dipped bread into a pool of olive oil. 'What business are you in?' he asked Frank.

I was in the crimson dress Frank had given me. He had bought me high heels to match, taking me to a store in Soho, having the salesman give him the shoes and then slipping them on me himself.

'Freight,' Frank said, resting his arm behind me on the leather banquette. At the bar, two women were drinking Cosmopolitans. The red was the color of rock candy with sun shining through it. 'Air freight.' He smiled at me the way a teacher might, when you had said something right.

A group of young men stood at the bar. They were drinking beer, all of them in suits, their shirts the color of grape or dark blue. They were like boys at Houghton, I thought, loud and laughing as if no one else were around. 'Bankers,' Frank said, seeing me looking at them. Their lips were smooth as if from lip balm.

'Where do you work, Frank?' Henry asked.

'Kennedy, Newark, LaGuardia.' A woman was walking up the spiral staircase. Her stiletto heels were red.

Frank poured us wine.

'Well,' Frank said. 'It's really good to meet Betsy's friends. Order whatever you want.' Sylvia glanced at me. 'Price is no object.' She started to laugh so I shook my head at her not to.

'Thanks, Frank,' I said.

'Though I would recommend the steak frites.'

We had steak frites.

'So, what do you do for fun?' Frank asked Henry, long fingers cupping his glass.

Henry sat up straight, his wrists against the table. 'Go to parties. Movies. Study.'

'What do you study?'

'I'm in high school.'

Frank moved his hand across my plate and took one of my fries.

'So, what do you study?'

'Math, English.'

'What level math?'

'Calculus.'

Frank nodded. 'That's good. Good for business. I was great at math, and physics. I ran my own business when I was in high school.'

'I didn't know that,' I said.

'Sure. All three boroughs.'

'Precocious,' Sylvia said.

'I pulled in $1,000 a week. Not bad for seventeen.'

'What were you doing?' Henry asked.

Frank laughed. 'Kid stuff.'

After the steak, we had salad. Frank speared lettuce on his fork. 'Let me guess what your father does,' he said to Henry.

'Sure.'

'He's not a dentist.'

'No.'

'Doctor, lawyer, banker.'

'My parents are bankers,' Sylvia told us.

'What kind?'

'Investment.'

'Very lucrative.'

'If you're good at it.'

'I assume they're good.'

Sylvia smiled.

'But back to Henry here.'

'He's a journalist,' Henry said.

'Newspaper?'

'Yes.'

'Which one?'

Henry motioned to the waiter that he was finished. 'Different ones,' he shrugged, holding up his hands. It was embarrassing to him that his father owned newspapers. He owned one in New York and one in London and a few smaller papers in Los Angeles and Singapore and Japan.

He flicked his hair from his eye. As usual, it was just a little too long. 'What are you interested in, Frank—besides work?'

'Well, I quite like Betsy here.'

'We know that,' Sylvia said. 'What about me?'

'What about you?' I asked.

'I don't see why the guys are talking about what they and their fathers do. What about us?'

'You're right,' Frank said. 'We will talk about you. Dessert, first?'

Sylvia took a dessert menu. 'Crème brûlée,' she decided, so Frank ordered four. 'I would like to teach.'

'Teach what?'

'English. Poetry. I like Plath.'

'Everyone likes Plath in high school,' Henry said. 'Do you want to be a cliché?'

'I don't like her,' I said.

'You do so.'

'I like some things, maybe.'

'You like that poem "Tulips."'

'I do like that.'

'The hospital poem,' Sylvia said. 'She didn't want flowers. She wanted to lie in bed and be empty.'

'Anyway,' Henry said, 'people act like she's the only poet in the world. It's ridiculous.'

'The point is, you want to teach,' Frank said to Sylvia.

'I think I'd be good.'

'Passion. That's the most important thing for a teacher, and you have that.'

Henry rolled his eyes at me, but I had to ignore him; Frank

noticed everything. He hailed a cab for Henry and Sylvia and tried to give Henry some money, but Henry wouldn't take it. 'Bye, Frank,' Sylvia called.

'She's sweet,' Frank said.

'I don't know about sweet.'

'He's got a problem, though.'

'What kind of problem?'

'I don't know. Insecurity, probably.'

I would have laughed. It was Frank who seemed insecure, bragging about how great he was in school. But I didn't laugh. You should never laugh at people, my mother said, especially not at men.

Inside the apartment, Frank pushed me the way you push a swinging door, his hand flat on my chest. I didn't have to fall. I could have righted myself. Falling was easiest, though, a slow deliberate giving way, a lying down. The pear wood floor was smooth. My hair was smooth on my back.

He wasn't rough this time, so much as cold. He was so cold, I thought I could die of it. That death itself had entered me, impersonal and final.

When he had finished, he staggered up and back from me, with his bare knees and black trouser socks. He pulled up his pants, his shirttail hanging out. Light fell on the low clouds so they looked like pools.

I took a throw from the couch and wrapped it around me. I heard the rustle of his clothes as he walked, the click of his belt when he hung it in his closet.

I heard the shower as he rinsed himself off. Then he stepped out, knotting a towel around his waist, opening the vanity cabinet. He washed his face with yellow soap, took out his pink tincture for his pale skin. He looked at himself as he flossed, at the lines around his eyes, the stain of wine on his tongue. He dropped the coil into the toilet where it spun in a wide circle.

'Frank?' I called.

His light went out. The duvet rustled, his legs lean with the muscles of a runner pushing down underneath his covers. Then there was nothing: hum of the refrigerator, idle cars in the street, the elevator going down, gears shifting. He wasn't coming back to me; I wasn't going to him, either. My voice was a bird in the hallway, desire an emptiness.

Later, it was still dark, I heard his bare feet, the bubbling of water from the water tank, the filling of a paper cone cup. He stood and drank, crumpling the cup and its waxy rim, dropping it to the wastebasket.

Then he came toward me, naked. I closed my eyes before he reached me.

I smelled his fresh skin and lemon soap. Then the blanket moved. The air moved—like water on my nakedness.

His fingers on my legs were warm. His tongue was like a rivulet: a cool, infinitely gentle, painstaking thing.

When I came, he went for a washcloth, white and heavy and hot with water. He pressed it to me, his fingers cupping me, thumb grazing my pubic hair.

'Did you like that?' he asked.

I knew better than to turn my face from him.

'Did you?' he pressed.

'Yes.'

He pulled me up, the throw falling soundless to the floor.

'Shall I carry you?'

I started walking. The floor was cold.

I tried to accept the hurt, to open up and not resist. That would make it easier, I thought. That would make it finish fast.

He didn't want to finish, though, his hands on the headboard. He went on and on, moving so hard I cried. I cried and I bled.

'Frank,' I said, and it was hot between my legs.

But he wanted it to hurt. That's what I realized. Finally, when he came, he pushed my head into the pillow, sideways, holding it there, the bones of his palm against my temple.

When he released me, I sat up, trying to inhale. I pulled the sheet around me and once I could breathe I started sobbing, and once I started I couldn't stop. I sobbed without restraint so he grabbed my wrist, the sheet falling and exposing my breasts.

Stop it, he said. *Stop it Stop it.* I wouldn't, though. I wouldn't and I wouldn't. My body ached from him. His mouth was sour at the corners. *Christ*, he said and he hated me. I saw hatred in him and then he slapped me, suddenly—slapped me so it felt as a branch does against your face when you are walking—so I froze for a second, I went completely quiet, and he got up.

He was gone a long time. His sheets were bloody. I didn't touch them or get up. I didn't move right or left. Finally, he sat beside me. He undid my fists. He curled out my fingers.

Outside, the sky was still dark. He gave me pills and a paper cone of cold water and he ran a bath. He lifted me into it, bath salts sharp on the bottom. He passed me a bar of wet soap and my hand shook so I dropped it on the marble floor and he said, 'Jesus Christ, Betsy,' and I started crying again, and he said, 'For fuck's sake,' sitting by the tub in his blue bathrobe and bare feet.

Eventually, he got up. I heard him strip the bed, I heard the washing machine. He lay down new sheets. 'Come on,' he said, helping me out of the bath, patting me down with one of his great, white towels.

He gave me a T-shirt and put me beside him in his bed and he didn't touch me again. He lay on his back, his chest moving slowly up and down, hands on his ribs.

It was noon when I woke. The lace panels were half open. 'Are you all right?' he asked, still lying beside me on the bed, now dressed in his black pants, white T-shirt, and white shirt.

I nodded.

'You lost control,' Frank told me, his voice flat and quiet.

Between the drapes, the sky was weak. Sun streaked the windows, which had dirt on them.

'Maybe I'm not good for you,' he went on.

'Don't say that.'

'I don't want to hurt you.'

'I know.'

'I hurt you last night.'

'You know what my brother said once?'

He didn't answer. His hands were on his chest again.

He said, 'I don't want to hurt you because if I hurt you, you'll bleed and they'll want to know why.'

Frank rolled his head to look at me. 'You need to eat,' he said.

When the delivery came, Frank set it on the coffee table by the couches: scrambled eggs and bacon and home fries, pancakes, coffee, and orange juice.

He made up a plate for me. He ate the bacon.

'It's two o'clock,' he said, putting on his polished shoes. 'I should get you home.'

'I'm not going home.'

'Where are you going?'

'To Sylvia's.'

'Then I'll take you to Sylvia's.'

Outside it was hot, a dry wind lifting dust from the gutters, light on the river darkening, then lightening.

'You're so quiet,' I said. His quiet made me nervous, made me suddenly want him—when the night before I had hated him.

'I'm tired.'

'But you're okay?'

He handed me his cell phone. 'Call your friend, make sure she's home.'

She was.

He stopped outside her building on 79th and Fifth. He opened the door for me, his eyes remote even as they rested on mine, the car still running.

'It's okay,' I said, 'isn't it?'

'Go on,' he said, not answering.

I don't know why I wanted him to call. Maybe I couldn't stand things ending so badly. I couldn't stand missing him and thinking about him and regretting all I had done. There had to be a way to make it right. Otherwise, I'd just have to live with it, to live with and live with it.

* * *

He didn't call that week. He didn't come to school. 'What's wrong with you?' Beck asked.

'You hardly talk,' Henry told me.

I called Frank's cell phone but he didn't pick up. I waited on Park Avenue but he didn't come. It was Monday when I reached him, from the pay phone after school. Sylvia was waiting for me. Frank was in his car. He always spoke loudly when he drove.

'What is it?' he asked.

'You didn't come.'

'I got tied up.'

'Are you coming this week?'

'Why?'

'Why?'

Silence came into the phone like static.

'I'll call you later.'

Sylvia watched me all careful when I hung up. She gave me this look my parents give me sometimes, as if I was going to do something crazy.

'What is it?' I asked.

She shook her head. 'Nothing.'

'What?'

'I don't know. Maybe Beck's better for you, that's all.'

Then he was outside school. He had the car running and started driving as soon as I got in. 'What's wrong?' I asked.

'Nothing.'

He didn't want to talk. He waved his hand with his wrist. He played Etta James, tapping his fingers on the steering wheel.

At home, he undid his shoes, his pants, and his shirt. He was erect. He ran his hand gently from the base to the tip. 'I missed you.'

He shouldn't have said that, not touching himself.

'Take off your clothes,' he said.

I lay naked beside him and he stroked my hair and maybe that was worth it, I thought. Just that. Him so calm and his hand on my hair. Afterwards, he lay on his back. 'It's not just that you're young.'

'What is it?'

'I'll hurt you.'

'You don't want to see me anymore?'

'I'm not a nice guy, Betsy.'

I thought I'd have to go to the bathroom. I didn't, though. 'That's such an odd thing to say. *I'm not a nice guy,*' I repeated. 'No one says that.'

My father played guitar. He played on our boat *Stewball* and he played in the garden and he played with my parents' friends in the living room. I could hear them from my room, singing 'Blue Moon' and 'Who's Sorry Now?' and 'Someday You'll Want Me to Want You.'

I called Frank from home and from school and from the street. 'Stop,' he told me.

'Stop what?'

'I'll call you when I can.'

He didn't, though. He didn't and he didn't and he didn't. Worse than that, I knew he wouldn't. My hands went cold just thinking about it. Beck came to school and it hurt each time I saw him, first because he wasn't Frank and second because I felt guilty, sick at myself for even thinking that way. I tried to be extra nice but I wasn't very good at it.

'This has to stop,' my mother said one Saturday morning, the second Saturday since Frank.

She brought a tray of food up to my room: eggs and two slices of toast and black jam. 'Is this about Beck?' She sat on the edge of the bed, pushing the tray toward me. The eggs were in wooden eggcups from Antigua. 'He seems like a nice boy.' She wore her hair straight and long, just past her shoulders. 'I'm not saying I think he's for you. I don't. But I can see why you like him.'

I took a sip of orange juice.

'Is it someone else?' she asked.

I would never tell my mother about Frank. She had seen him and she hadn't liked him. He was the kind of guy, as I said, who would look at you on the street—and my mother didn't like those men either. She looked away from them, her mouth pursed. 'You couldn't blame them for trying,' she said.

'Sort of,' I said.

She would have told me not to see Frank again, if I told her anything. It would sound so easy.

'Well, I can't make you talk if you don't want to. But you can if you want to.'

She looked around the room. 'You know, we should get you a new rug. Something more grown up.'

I called Frank again, of course, the way everyone said not to— Sylvia and Henry and my mother and Beck of course if I had asked him. 'It's not a good time,' he told me.

'When is a good time?'

'I'll call you.'

It was like I was lying on the ground and something heavy was on my chest. At school, rain flooded the windows, streaming down the slick panes, into the flutes, down the gutters.

'There's always another guy,' Sylvia said, walking home down Fifth Avenue, underneath her great black umbrella.

'There is not.'

'You didn't even like him.'

'I liked him.'

'*Love is a shadow, how you lie and cry after it.*'

'Plath?'

'"Elm."'

At night in my room, the light of the streetlamp fell whitely on the tree, coolly on the sheets. I saw Frank stroking my hair before we made love, Beck singing in the playground. I saw Andrew, who waited at the school gates. His father owned a fish shop. He took me beneath the schoolhouse, or to the rough shore by the whitened trees. Andrew worked at the dockyard, his hands dry from the sun and salt.

I liked the dark best: cool stones at the dockyard, slate rocks by the ocean, fetid soil under the schoolhouse.

* * *

Get up Get up Get Up, my father said, raising the wood blinds so they slapped against each other, sun whitening the walls. *Macavity Macavity, there's no one like Macavity. There never was a cat of such deceitfulness and suavity.* He wasn't the man who picked me up from the front porch of the house, beside the lemon tree in his creased cream white shirt. He wasn't the man who turned the pages, sitting sleepy beside my bed. He hardly knew me—knew nothing of Ray and Beck and Frank—knew only that he was suspicious of me, eyeing me coolly, asking suddenly and too late, 'What's going on?'

My mother said, 'Stop it. Stop it. She's just a girl. She's just. She's just—'

I heard them from my room, their voices carrying up the stairs. 'All girls go through it, don't they? Don't they?'

Then one day he sat down on the bed. The sun made him squint. His skin smelled of shaving cream. 'You can't keep moping around the house.' The blinds were swinging at the top of the windows, after he had snapped them. His leg touched mine. 'You think it only affects you?' he asked. 'We all have to live with it. Your mother and Eric and me. Your mother thinks you're unhappy about this boy Beck. Is that true?'

Even though he was my dad, he was still handsome: his even face, dark hair, dark blue eyes.

'We thought you'd be happier with Raymond gone. We knew he made things difficult for you. But no one's upsetting you now, are they?'

'No.'

'So what is it?'

I couldn't think of anything.

'You don't talk to anyone. You're rude to your mother.'

He was wearing his Saturday clothes: pressed jeans and a crimson sweater, the collar of a white shirt just showing.

'Can you say? Can you say anything?'

It was so long ago: light of the moon streaking down the cockpit hatch, water slapping against the hull, nipping like fish. Ray smelled of toothpaste. He had the sheet in his hand.

'What are you doing?' Dad had asked, stepping from the shadows and the silence of the foredeck, from the silence of my mother sleeping.

'Nothing,' Ray said.

'Betsy?'

And there it was: complicity—beginning of the endless lie.

'Nothing.'

'I can't hear you,' Dad said, leaning in, me straightening my back against the wall.

I shook my head. I hadn't said anything.

'Speak up.'

He didn't know anything. He looked tired suddenly—and disappointed. 'Stay at school if you can't be pleasant. Or stay in your room.'

He had a small mouth, or it went small when he was angry.

'I'd like to go away,' I said. 'I'd like to go to boarding school.'

'Why?'

'To get away from Beck.'

'What has Beck done?' I shook my head. 'You think if you go away, you'll escape this boy? But what about the next one? Have you thought about that? What will you do then?'

'It won't be the same.'

'But it will. It will be just the same.'

'You don't know.'

'Why would I send away my only daughter? Because she doesn't like some boy anymore?'

'It's not him.'

'You just said it was.'

I couldn't explain.

He sighed. 'I'm going downstairs. If you helped your mother around the house, I'm sure she'd like it.'

'I'd like to go to boarding school.'

'Well, you're not going.'

Beck let me sit on the bench while he played ball. My whole body got pins and needles worrying Frank might come.

'Where've you been?' Tommy asked, and I said, 'Nowhere.'

'Oh yeah?' he asked, smirking. 'Is that right?'

'That's right.'

Beck was mad at me, of course. He had walked over to the fence real slow when I showed up the first time, like it was a great effort for him. He took me back, though—not because he wanted to, he said, not because he wasn't angry, but because he still liked me.

He didn't come to school the way he had before Frank. He didn't sing 'She's the One,' or get down on his knees and kiss my hand. I sat on the bench as he shot the ball and he didn't look at me at all.

Then one day, finally, Frank drove up, and Beck must have seen him the way he always had, but he kept on playing as if he hadn't. Frank got out of his car, laying his long hands on his hips. When he saw me, it was like I was nothing at all. I was less than that—because he'd seen me once and tried me out and put me back. He didn't smile at me or even register that he had seen me, so I thought I might throw up. I went all weak and chilled and I remembered this ferry I had once seen sunk in the ocean: the way it had been emptied out and they opened the valves, and as it started to sink suddenly, I imagined all the water, cold and dark and heavy, filling the hull.

'Take it easy,' Tommy said, and on the ground was a circle of blue gum embedded in the black tar and a glint of glass and I put my hand to my forehead. 'He's gone,' Tommy told me, and I couldn't get up because Beck would be upset, so I turned away, from Tommy and the court and Beck. Trees were waving before the clean white brownstones. Tommy stepped next to me. 'Hey,' he said, 'hey,' and he touched the back of my neck. 'I'll get Beck,' he said.

'No,' I told him and wiped my face again, keeping my eyes down, and I sat that way, not moving at all, not hearing anything or hardly seeing, my heart beating high up in my chest, and then it passed.

Sylvia and Henry broke up senior year. Sylvia wanted to go out to the clubs, but Henry didn't. He said she should go and he would meet her afterwards. Then she got a new boyfriend. He was a bartender at the Madison Pub. He was twenty-two and had been to the Rhode Island School of Design. Sylvia gave him a set of her keys and he came over after work. They went to clubs downtown and drove to Jersey City where he had an apartment.

Wayne moved to New York that year. He and my mother sat in the garden drinking white wine. I watched them from the window: my mother's white blond hair shining in the afternoon light, his body stretched out in his garden chair, wine glass on the metal armrest.

Beck graduated and got into the Marines finally. He went in the fall and didn't write at all. He called from boot camp in Virginia. He said, 'Hey, girl, who's the one who's loved you since, like, forever?'

'You are.'

'You thought I'd forgotten you, right?'

'No.'

''Cause, like, that ain't ever going to happen.'

He was eating potato chips. I could hear the crackling of his packet. 'Like, never. You know. 'Cause I'm, like, your destiny.'

I laughed.

'No don't fucking laugh, 'cause it's true.'

Then he went quiet. He was probably remembering Frank.

'What are you doing?' I asked.

'I've got this phone card.'

'Do you like the Marines?'

'You like it—it's fucking over.'

'What do you mean?'

'I mean, Betsy, I hate it. I fucking hate it. Excuse my language.'

'That's terrible,' I said.

'Yeah, well—whatever.'

* * *

Henry and I went to the reservoir after school, him in his running pants with a packet of Gauloise cigarettes in his pocket. He hardly ever smoked, but Sylvia's new boyfriend did so Henry had been trying to. We walked the bridle path where the dirt was dark and soft and moist, the trees high and thick as they are in England. Only some kinds of people could go from one person to another, Henry said, and Sylvia was one of those.

In the spring, we took the subway to the Brooklyn Botanic Garden. The tulips were flowering red and gold and pale blue, and Henry took the photo that he later sent me at Fairley. Young orthodox couples sat on benches under the elm trees, the girls' hair shiny and loosed and brushed.

Henry pressed the fruit of the maple seed with his thumb. 'Do you ever think about us going out?'

'Sure.'

'What do you think?'

His eyes were the brown of polished wood. 'I think it would be nice,' I said.

The maple seed split under his thumbnail. 'But . . . ?' Henry asked.

'But what?'

'But you wouldn't really want to.'

'Maybe I would. I just—'

'You just what?'

'Look at Frank.'

'You're not seeing Frank, are you?'

'I still like him.'

'You don't like him.'

'No?'

'You like me.'

He looked at the maple seed as if at an insect he had just crushed.

I wished I could go out with Henry. I wished he would just lean over and kiss me. At the same time, I knew that if he did, I would move away.

'That's true,' I finally said.

'But you're not over him?'

It wasn't that either.

What it was—and what Henry didn't know because I didn't tell him—was that just the thought of Frank made my whole body hurt, that just a glimpse of him, real or imagined, of his dark hair or his leather blazer or his pressed shirt, made me sick inside. What Henry didn't know was that none of these things ever happened with Henry and I didn't desire him.

⟶

I studied late at night, when no one else was up. I had my books and notepads and pens all lined up. I made up index cards with information on them and carried them about in a red card folder. I still wanted to be a doctor, though I didn't study enough. I didn't concentrate. I got up and walked around my room and hung pictures and photographs on my walls: trees and the sea and photographs of Sylvia and Henry and me. My favorite photo was of Antigua: Eric and me sitting on the steps of the house, him in a green T-shirt, me in a blue dress my mother had made for me. Raymond was above us, leaning back against a pillar, his mouth turned down as if someone had just insulted him.

Some nights, I stayed up until morning. I lifted my window and sat on the ledge. The brownstones across the street were dark inside. Then day began to glow and the birds came out.

⟶

In May I came out of school, and there he was: not leaning against a car, not holding some orange soda or cigarette, but upright in a uniform that was stiff as cardboard, tailored.

'Jesus,' Henry said as Beck took off his hat.

His hair was even shorter than usual. His shoes were shiny and big like the shoes of a child. Then he winked and it was as if I remembered him, in that moment, as if he moved inside my skin like hot sun. He picked me up, carrying me down the street the way men carry women in old movies.

'What do you think?' he asked, setting me down, pointing to his uniform all bashful like the day we met. 'You like it?'

He wanted me to like it. He wanted it so much, I smiled at him. 'Yes, I like it.'

'I thought you would. I thought, you know, I'd come up here and surprise you.'

'You did.'

'I make you nervous, right?'

'A little.'

'I make everyone nervous.'

'You look good.'

'You think?'

People stared at him. We walked down Lexington and people turned to look. The green of his uniform brought out the color of his eyes. The shade of his Marine hat made them look deeper. He didn't smoke anymore, he said, not in the street, not when he was in uniform. 'It doesn't look right,' he told me, 'throwing the butt in the gutter.'

'Hey. Look,' I said. 'This is where we met.'

It was 79th Street, the crosstown bus billowing black smoke.

He took me by the shoulders, moving me over to the wall.

'I missed you so fucking much.'

He acted like we were as close as ever sometimes, like months didn't go by without us seeing each other, even when we were both in the city.

'Can we go to your house?'

'Now?'

'Just for a little while.'

'Okay.'

It was dark and quiet in the hallway. I poured him a Coke in the kitchen, with cubes of ice.

'Can we go upstairs?' Beck asked.

'To my room?'

'I've never seen it. I've never seen your fucking room.'

'My mother's coming home.'

'Come on.'

He took off his shoes at the foot of the stairs. He carried his hat in his hands.

'So here it is.'

The blinds were still down from morning. I crossed the carpet to raise them. 'Don't,' Beck said, coming from behind me, putting his arms around me. 'I've dreamt about this room.'

The collar of his wool uniform pricked my skin.

Something was gone between us, like the warm part of day. He had hardened himself up. Maybe he'd done it so he could stand me, so he could still be with me.

Afterwards, I opened the slats of the blind with my hand. I listened to the sounds of the house, making sure no one had come in. 'Why do you hate the Marines?'

His arm across mine was heavy and damp. He smelled of sweat and something slightly burnt.

'It's just killing and more killing. That's all anyone talks about.'

'You're unhappy?'

'Fuck yeah.'

'Can you get out?'

'No.'

He lay on his back. 'You know how often I imagined this room?'

'A lot?'

'Yes. Are you going to college?'

'Probably.'

I touched his stomach and he tightened his muscles, so they were hard as rope.

I thought of Frank's apartment, of his cream and crimson sheets and waking up early in the morning to pale gray cloud all around the building. 'Do you still see Frank?' I asked.

'Frank?'

'Yes.'

'He's around.' He ran his fingers across his abdomen. 'He goes out with some Asian girl. A banker type.'

My jeans were at the end of the bed. I stood up and pulled

them on. I went to the bureau for a fresh T-shirt. 'What about Tommy?'

Beck dropped his head into the pillow. Then he turned his cheek. 'He's the same.'

'And Seth?'

'In jail.'

'Really?'

'Something with Frank.'

I sat on my desk chair, pulling on my socks. 'But Frank's not in jail?'

'No.'

'You should get up,' I said, looking at the door. 'My mother's coming home.'

'I like it here.'

I smiled. 'Do you?'

'Come over here. Please.'

I moved beside him, on the edge of the bed. He touched my breasts under my T-shirt.

'Beck.'

'What?'

'My mother's coming home.'

He undid the button on my pants. 'Get up,' I said.

'Not yet.'

'Please.'

When the front door opened, he pulled my body onto him. 'Let go,' I said. He started to pull down my pants but then stopped.

'I'll always come back, Betsy. You do know that?'

When we came downstairs, my mother was still in the kitchen, a glass of wine on the table. 'Beck.' She opened her eyes wide. 'I was wondering who was here.'

'I just showed him the house.'

'I saw his shoes.'

'He didn't want to get anything dirty.'

'So you're a Marine now.'

'Yes, ma'am.'

'Well, I suppose if you're a Marine I can offer you a beer.'

All the times I would have liked to have Beck over, to have my parents give him a drink, suddenly were gone. Beck drank his beer from the bottle, his beautiful full mouth and freckles on his cheekbones. My mother leaned back against the kitchen counter. She was wearing a cream silk dress, a shirt dress open at the neck, and high heels. I liked that she was beautiful. I liked being proud of her when she came to school. She got enough attention, though. She didn't need to slip off her shoe the way she did, to slide her slim ivory-stockinged foot in and out of it, cocking her hip, holding up her wineglass beside her pale blue eyes.

'We have to go,' I said.

Henry was accepted to Princeton. His father had gone there and his grandfather and his great-grandfather so there wasn't much he could do not to get in, he said. At the reservoir, an Indian man was selling shaved ice with flavoring.

'Why go where your father went?' I asked.

'If I don't go there it'll be just as much his influence.'

'Except that it will be your own school.'

'Except that,' Henry laughed, his raspberry ice dripping on his hand. 'I wouldn't get in anywhere as good—'

'Sure you would.'

'My grades are mediocre. My SAT scores are passable. It's Princeton or bust.' He laughed again. Our fathers were the same kind, Henry said. 'They know everything. They have to prove that they know everything and they won't relax until you think they know everything.'

'You like your dad.'

'I do. I just wish he'd let me have a different opinion than he does.'

'On what?'

'Anything. No matter what I do, he looks at it as having to do specifically with him. If I go to Princeton, it's because he went to Princeton. If I go to New Orleans and become, say, a fisherman, it's because I'm running away from him to become a fisherman.'

'Then you have to not care.'

'But I do care.' Henry ran his fingers through his hair, helping it to stick up. 'That's what's so annoying.'

He went to Princeton and Sylvia to Bennington and I went to Sarah Lawrence. It was thirty minutes from the city, in Bronxville, quiet and green with acres of woods. Sometimes I had a notion that Frank would drive up and wait outside for me. Probably he didn't even know where I was. Beck went to Lebanon and got dysentery and was hot and bored and sick of everybody. My dorm room at Sarah Lawrence was small and narrow and we slept together there once, snow on the trees. There was this great space that kept growing between us and part of that was Frank and the other part was just who we were.

I went to visit Henry at Princeton. It was winter, snow deep on the lawns and libraries and bare trees. Henry and I dressed in his down jackets and wool hats and his L.L. Bean boots. We went to a party and drank rum and Coke. On the way home we lay in the snow outside his dorm, and I liked Henry more than I had ever liked anyone. Up in his room, he kissed me on his bed and I felt a great affection for him and I also felt like crying, because I didn't desire him, at all.

We slept together all that winter, in his dorm room in New Jersey and mine in Bronxville. Before he left for class, he made me cups of tea. He put on music and cracked the window for the icy air to wind in like ribbon. I could smell buttered toast and one day, I thought, I would break through my coldness—and it would work out.

He was the first person I ever told about Raymond. I thought it might make him feel better about me being in love with Frank and not with him. Maybe it did, too, for a while. He said, 'Jesus, Betsy, that's the key.' In the end, though, it was the same. His fingertips on my breast irritated me. When he kissed my mouth, I turned my head. Later, he said he couldn't do it anymore, he felt useless and it was no good for either of us. I sat on his futon and cried—not just over him, but over his dorm room and his batik bedspread and the way he put on music for me, left a cup of tea for me whenever he went out. Those were things real boyfriends did; with a real boyfriend, you slept in his dorm and made eggs in the morning or went out with other people your age for french toast at three a.m. Henry and I did these things.

'But you love me and everything,' I said. 'You told me.'

'I know.'

'So what does that mean?'

'Oh, come on, Betsy,' he said, sitting on the floor beside me, his arms on his knees. 'Don't make things worse.'

I wanted to. I didn't love him the way I wanted to, but he still could have tried harder. I would have tried.

PART IV

I HAVE 'TREATMENT' at the end of June. Kenneth drops me off at the conference center and it is not unlike the Last Supper with all the staff in a row: Keats in the center, Nurse Caroline on his right, and Lindsey from Morning Group on his left. Then there is Robert, my drug counselor, Thomas the nutritionist, and Ellie from Eating Disorders. There is Vicki, the meds nurse, and a few others I do not know.

I sit in a wooden chair, a few feet back. The windows are level with the tops of the trees. Sunlight lies on the wood floor. Adam is a nurse's aide and sets out clear plastic cups. He is twenty-three and handsome and going to medical school in the fall. I am wearing a red skirt my friend Robbie bought me at the gift shop and an oversized white sweater. The sweater was a mistake, first because all the Eating Disorder girls wear oversized shirts, and second because it is hot.

Keats takes off his blue blazer, beads of dust floating in the amber light. 'Elizabeth Scott, known to us as Betsy,' he says, opening a folder thick with lab tests and nurses' notes, 'came to Fairley on April 25, having that morning been picked up by the police in Central Park. She spent her first twenty-eight days in Substance Abuse and is now in Adult Psychiatric.'

I like it when he says *Adult Psychiatric*. I have finally arrived, I think, at a place where I should be. Outside, Adam is now crossing the lawn, on his way back to Main House. His hair is curly and dark. He has a girlfriend his own age, I imagine, someone who plays tennis or lacrosse.

My progress has been excellent, Keats says. I have completed the Substance Abuse program. I have remained sober and reached target weight. Robert leans back in his chair, his skin red and blotchy as if he still drinks. 'That's all great,' he says, opening his hands. 'It really is, and I think Betsy's doing great also. But she does seem to be on a lot of medication.'

He says this as if he has said it before, about other people.

'She has left Group twice this week,' Lindsey says.

The first time I left Group, rising from my pink upholstered and chrome metal chair, pushing through the swinging glass doors past the indoor swimming pool and the gift shop with its jewelry and leisure clothes, I thought someone would catch up with me—that some nurse or guard or our counselor Lindsey would take me by the shoulders and turn me around, take me back to my seat. Instead, I made it through the front doors of Rec. and Kenneth was there, standing by the Lincoln Continental in his thin black tie.

'Are you okay?' he asked, his hair white and lightly waxed.

'Yes.'

He shook out his cigarettes for me. Across from Rec., in front of Dobson House, the breeze played with the dandelions. A white birch shone like rope. Kenneth held up his silver lighter, '*K Lundon*' engraved on the side.

In the car, Kenneth drove with his window down. The trees were still fresh with dew, the sun distant from the earth. Up at Main House, Vicki called Dr. Keats and then gave me Klonopan, a small, chalky orange pill the color of a Creamsicle. I took a cup of ice and a carton of orange juice and lay out on the grass. I liked Klonopan. Klonopan laid me out—as on a beach, on a hot towel receiving sun.

Since then, I have left Group six times. This is almost twice a week, Keats says, and too much. He would like to lower my medication, but first I need to sit through Group, to be less 'labile.' It is then decided that I am generally well liked, have made several friends amongst the patients and staff, and am particularly active in occupational and recreational therapies. I am regularly seen, Sammy says, at the swimming pool.

Keats smiles at me, in his soft, quiet, deliberate way. 'How do you feel about your treatment here?'

'How do I feel?'

Sammy's eyes flick to the windows and back. She is twenty-five and has a degree in Stress Management. She has red hair and a pretty face, smooth and placid as on a Greek vase.

'I feel,' I say, slipping my hands beneath my thighs, palms against the slats of the wooden chair, 'that everyone always thinks I'm doing well.'

'And you don't think so?' Keats asks.

A Philippine maid is carrying sheets into Bishop House, her hair in a dark bun shining like corn syrup.

Nurse Caroline leans in toward me. 'People judge you on your outsides, don't they?' she asks me. 'Rather than your insides.'

I hate that kind of language. Anyway, she has it mixed up. '*Don't compare your insides to other people's outsides*,' that's what it's supposed to be.

'Maybe.'

'No one is suggesting that you're ready to leave,' Dr. Keats says. 'Is that what you're afraid of?' His eyes are not stunning. His eyes are not the brilliant green of water in Antigua, not blue as the sky or azure—yet they are startling to me, open yet serious.

'I guess it is.'

Afterwards, Kenneth walks me to the car. I light a cigarette. Smoke fills my lungs like water.

'How did it go?'

'Okay.'

'They helping you any?'

'Maybe.'

We stop beside the car. Dr. Keats comes out with Sammy. Wind blows her red hair into her mouth and the tops of the oak trees sway.

'You've got to want it,' Kenneth says, stamping out his stub.

'To want what?'

'To be well.'

The truth is, nobody but Dr. Keats and Wayne would ever admit I wasn't well. Maybe Raymond had caused my parents enough grief; maybe he was all the grief my parents could stand. The day the police picked me up, at 5:22 a.m. in Central Park, in the West 70s by the lake's edge, my parents were asleep in their yellow cotton sheets, pale sun rising on the second floor, on their large quiet room beneath Raymond's room, on the bluish garden. It was my father who rose and dressed, who took a cab in his gray suit to the police station where I sat with my coffee cup, with a lieutenant in a white shirt with thick crimson stripes, yellow stain like an iron burn beside the middle button; he pushed up my shirtsleeve when my father came, showing him my track marks like bruises, blue and yellow deep inside the skin.

Outside, it was too bright. My lungs hurt. In the cab, my father leaned against the far door, his handsome face all tight as if in a hard wind. 'I'm sorry,' I said in this voice so quiet and grave I almost stopped breathing. He was like Wayne, though. He had too much going on in himself. 'Not now,' he warned and held up his hand, looking out at Central Park as the cab moved through it.

Inside the house, it smelled of fresh coffee and freesia and furniture polish. My mother was in her dressing gown and sat beside me on the bed, her skin in the dim yellow light of spring soft, like that of her mother, who I never knew but was English and didn't go in the sun. 'What is going on?' she asked.

My father sat by the window, in their blue armchair. Slim trees eased their way up from the garden. 'Show her your arms.'

'Dad—'

My mother pushed up my sleeve. I saw a flicker like a tic in the soft skin under her eye. 'Charming.' That wasn't the reaction I expected. 'Where is your brother?' she asked.

'I don't know.'

'Don't you care?'

I did and I didn't.

My parents have always had nice bathrooms. In Antigua, they had had their bathroom tiles shipped from England. In New York, their tub was pink granite, the light dim, rose-colored from the walls. My mother hung a dress on the back of the door: one of my old dresses, a shirt dress with long sleeves and a belt. She folded a pair of underwear on the counter, peach colored with a lace band at the top.

'I don't understand it,' she said.

I sat up in the tub, so water splattered on the floor. I had a bath sponge in my hands, in the shape of a heart. She leaned against the doorway, her bare ankle cocked in her high-heeled slipper.

'You have everything. What could you possibly want in your life?'

'It's not about that.'

'What is it about?'

She knew what it was about. 'Just because—' she said.

'Just because *what?*'

The sponge was heavy in my hands.

'It's Ray or it's Beck or it's Wayne. When are you responsible?'

Certain times—times at Fairley, times after Beck or Frank, at the very end of things—the world grows so quiet I lie on my bed with my palms up. I look out the window at the spreading trees, and the gold light on the bark is gold like a wedding band, only cold.

My father drives from the city and is late for Session. He is close-shaven, his face and body lean with ambition. He walks fast through Reception so people look at him. 'Hello, Betsy,' he says in his cool, deliberate, cautious way. He is so angry, and I can't understand it. He will do anything for Raymond: bail him out of jail, get him into schools, hire lawyer after lawyer. But when it comes to me, he is tired already.

'It's as if he hates me,' I tell Keats.

'Hate is a strong word.'

'That's how it feels.'

'He does seem uncomfortable with you.'

'Uncomfortable?'

'He has trouble dealing with you.'

'He deals with Raymond.'

'He helps Raymond. That's not the same as dealing with him.'

Keats holds his hands in his lap—smooth, square,

unblemished hands. 'You're emotional. It threatens some people.'

In high school, Keats was probably a really nice person. He wouldn't have been a school star, but he wouldn't have been an underdog either. I probably wouldn't have talked to him at all.

'Sometimes,' I tell Keats, 'I think Dad treats Raymond differently because he's the oldest son.'

'You think your father favors him?'

'Yes.'

'How?'

'Just the way he makes excuses for him—as if he can do no wrong, as if he is an extension of my father.'

'But you're not?'

'No.'

'Because you're a girl?'

'I don't know. It could be part of it. Raymond can do anything he wants, say anything he wants, treat me any way he wants—and Dad will still defend him.'

'But he doesn't defend you?'

'He's paying for me to be in the hospital.'

'So he cares.'

I smile. 'He cares.'

'But not as much as he does for Raymond?'

I shrug.

'Where does that leave you?'

'Talking to you.'

I sit with the alcoholics, usually, at a long table in an alcove by the window. I am not an alcoholic, but I might as well be. I am not supposed to drink again. Robbie isn't either and he is here for Xanax. After dinner, we go down to the porch at Rec. and play guitar. He plays 'Angie' and beads of sweat gather above his lip; his bright red polo shirt grows dark with sweat.

*

My last year at Sarah Lawrence, Wayne got me my job at World Sight. He had been there for three years by then and was a director of overseas programs. He sent doctors into Africa, mostly, to give cataract operations. I worked in fundraising for the sight unit in Kenya. Every Friday, I took the train from Sarah Lawrence to Penn Station, walking up to 42nd Street and across to the river. I was applying to medical schools and Wayne helped me with my personal essay and the MCAT admissions test. We went over to the East River in the afternoons, Wayne sneaking one of his four daily cigarettes, and he asked me questions off my notecards.

Other times, he asked me about Henry and Beck. 'You were there,' I told him. 'You were there during Beck.'

'That's true.'

'Do you remember that?'

'I remember that you were upset.'

'That wasn't just Beck.'

'Wasn't it?'

I told him about Frank then, though maybe I shouldn't have. It was gray by the river, and his face turned gray, also.

'You think I'm awful,' I said.

'I don't.'

'You do.'

'I don't think he's so great.'

'No.'

'You could go out with anyone you wanted.'

'No, I couldn't.'

'Of course you could.'

'Frank stopped seeing me. So did Henry.'

'Frank sounds like a weakling.'

'A weakling?' Frank was not a weakling.

'And Henry was your choice.'

'No, it wasn't.'

Wayne shook his head. 'Does your mother know all this?'

'I don't think so.'

'She never mentioned it.'

'No.'

'She broke some hearts, too.'

I laughed. 'Did she? You're not in love with her, are you?'

'Everyone is in love with your mother.'

'Because she's beautiful?'

'She is that.'

My mother had only one affectation: an awareness of her own beauty, a certain self-consciousness when being watched or photographed. Wayne reached out and put his hand on the back of my neck.

'You're not jealous of your mother, are you, Betsy?'

'No.'

'You should be proud.'

'I am.'

'Of yourself, too.'

I laughed.

I was proud, in some ways. Or maybe I was vain. It was like that time, the first time with Frank, and he said I was beautiful like Christ was. I knew I wasn't, of course. But I let him say it. There was something else, too, something as important as beauty, something no one could define, no one could be sure of. In Antigua, I just had to look at Andrew and he knew how I felt. One minute I was walking out of school with Angie Edwards, our sandals kicking up dust, our hands filled with hot coins on our way to buy candy. The next, I saw Andrew leaning against a fence and everything changed. Everything went weak inside me. My yellow dress, yellow cotton dress of my school uniform, went hot like a body on a beach; I was full of heat and sun, heavy and soft and languid with it.

After Frank, I thought I'd never be with anyone again. That would have been the best thing for me, I'm sure, at least for a while. It kind of amazed me that that wasn't the case. Things kept happening, though. I said I didn't want them to, but I must have, because they did.

I met Curtis at a dance in Princeton, Henry right there in the room. I gave him my number and he drove out to see me the next afternoon. We went to his parents' house on Long Island. They were in Florida and we lay beside the house, at night on the cool grass where he used his tongue on me.

Adam liked movies. He took me to the Thalia and Film Forum. He wanted me to touch him in the train, and the theater, but I wouldn't. Afterwards, he came up to my room and he was the gentlest, like water on a rock, so slow it felt like forever.

Thomas could have been my greatest love: tall and slim and with the kindest eyes I had ever seen, so I felt like crying sometimes, just seeing his face. He loved to drink screwdrivers and send the ice back and forth between our mouths. He was from Cold Spring Harbor and he was seeing someone from there.

Bad guys just groped you wherever they liked. Good guys put their hands on your hips, so delicately you felt sorry for them.

After graduation, I moved to 46th Street, and Paul was the first person I ever took home. We met at the Coliseum Bookstore. He was an acting student, and also a fencer. He had his foil with him and jumped around my room with it, showing me how to joust. He took me to his parents' house also, in Forest Hills.

Richard was a researcher at World Sight. He was thirty and crazy about me, but only if it was 'just lust,' he said.

Sometimes, after a bad experience, I called up Beck and he came over and said all his nice things about loving me forever. He didn't, really. Even he must have known this. Sometimes I think he stayed in touch with me because I was still from the only rich parents he knew. We had never even gone to a movie together. We had never even had dinner.

I got into medical schools in Boston and in Maryland. I didn't get in in New York, though, and I didn't want to leave. I liked my apartment and I liked World Sight.

It was Wayne who suggested that I defer for a year.

The day after Raymond came home, after the airport and dinner at Sardi's, Wayne and I were at the river by the UN leaning against the bright railing.

'So how did he seem?'

'Quiet.'

'He's probably terrified.'

'You think?'

'Coming back here? I'd say so. What did you do after dinner?'

'I went home.'

'I'm surprised they let you.'

'A friend came over.'

'Oh, really?' Wayne laughed. 'Who was that?'

I shook my head.

'Oh, come on,' he said. 'You can tell me.'

'Beck.'

'Really?' He raised his eyebrows. 'Good for you.'

'I guess.'

After his first wife died, Wayne had years of girlfriends: doctors, nurses, teachers, bankers. I felt sorry for them sometimes, the way Wayne and my parents sat in the living room and discussed them, the way my mother always, in the end, outshone and outlasted them. When I was sixteen, Wayne married Ida, a German woman who lived in Belgium. She had a son who was four, named Marcus. My parents went over for the wedding. Ida was older than Wayne, my mother said, and 'not a great beauty.' She was the director of a hospital, though; they had a lot in common, and it 'worked for them,' my mother said—their long-distance marriage.

Later, it occurred to me that Wayne's marriage may have worked for my mother, but it didn't work so well for Wayne—Ida in Belgium, Wayne in New York or Africa. He spent the last week of each month in Belgium. But he was unhappy there and unhappy in New York. He told me this in his office and by the river and at *Le Balcon*.

Ray stepped into my life as into an empty space. He was, as I said, completely changed, deferential, as if, in his long absence, his family had become unreal to him, mythical or ideal, and in this state I was his Sister, capital S, who would not forsake him. We went to Glide and to Shelby's and to a local bar on Ninth Avenue. We went to my apartment, sitting at the kitchen table on the airshaft. Ray emptied out the pockets of his jacket: cigarettes and keys and tea-tree-oil toothpicks, crumpled bills and matchbooks. He pulled a translucent packet, plastic and taped, from his black combat boot. We played music and backgammon and it wasn't the way it had been with Sylvia; we were older, and Raymond knew more than I, and one night he moved his shiny red checker across the white and green backgammon board and asked if I wanted to try something new.

'New like what?' I asked.

The pupils of his eyes were black and fine as pins. His shirtsleeves were unbuttoned and I could see his pale wrists, veiny blue at the center. He took the cocaine into the kitchen and put a saucepan on the stove. He used baking soda and cooked up the coke until it turned, like sugar, hard and into rocks.

'Sit down,' he said, and kneeled before me.

He held his lighter so the flame went deep inside the pipe, the rocks of cocaine glowing red as he inhaled and then he handed the pipe to me, watched as I held it to my lips.

I went to Wayne's office after work and he had his feet up on the desk, his head turned to look out the window. The sun was pale and pink on the gray river, the coffee table littered with coffee cups and bottled water and newspapers.

'Are you all right?' Wayne set down the phone.

I could smell dirt and water and a fresh wind across the river. 'I am.'

He leaned toward me, into his desk. 'You look sort of—waxy.'

'Do I?'

I couldn't eat when I was with Ray. He called from pay phones and from his cell phone and from our parents' house, and his voice was quiet, almost diffident, a voice I had never heard from him before, but that was steady, close, that gave me relief and release into some kind of peace. He waited outside World Sight and we walked west to a cash machine and then further, across 41st Street to Eleventh Avenue and a yellow brick building that looked, always, as if the sun had just set on it, which perhaps it had—sheen fading on the far Hudson River. The super had a chair set up under a row of buzzers and wore a pale blue shirt, '*Jesus*' written in red letters inside a white oval patch.

Ray was so nervous; he stepped back and forth, back and forth, in his black jeans and boots, gripping his arms with his hands. If Frank were there, he would have swung up to that building in his massive car, with his white collar and leather blazer and scenic smile, and he would have been in and out of that place in about thirty seconds. Ray just stood there, talking and smoking with Jesus. Finally, we stepped into the building, into a freight elevator that was metal and smelled of dogs. The floor was dirty blue linoleum, and in the basement, Jesus held open the elevator door with his body, while Raymond talked to the dealer. 'Your boyfriend?' he always asked me. He was from Mexico City. His eyes were brown with gold flecks. He winked at me so I felt warm inside, like maybe he liked me.

Like hard rain on a hot deck, that's what the rush was like. Like light moving through night sky and burning color through it—or the space left in your chest after sound passes.

At four a.m., the sky in the city was not even dark, but rose-colored, city lights thrown into the hazy cloud. At five, morning had already arrived, pale and yellow like the underside of an animal at the side of the road.

I washed my face and Raymond wore his sunglasses and it was like sleepwalking with your eyes open, so you were moving through a landscape that was loud and bright and without any space for you, yet at the same time it hardly touched you.

I went to Wayne's office after lunch and he was working at his desk.

'Hey.' He was glad to see me.

He put down his pencil. He always used pencils, always sharp. 'How are you?' he asked.

I saw his long slim fingers, his blue shirt turned over at the cuffs, dark blond hair on his forearms. Sunlight moved from lattice to windowpane.

'Okay.'

His mouth was naked like a boy's, but more expressive. He had never done cocaine with his sister or anyone.

His hand was gentle as the hand that rested on my mother's back at Shirley Heights, on the smooth yellow stones under the colored lights. I stood at the metal lattice window looking out, the stone ledge up to my waist.

'Shouldn't you be working?' he asked.

'I should.'

'Look at that.' He came and stood beside me, watching a yawl tack up the East River.

I took Wayne's hand and pressed it to my hip.

'Jesus,' he said, 'is that your bone?'

'Yes.'

'Don't you eat?'

I didn't much.

'Don't you care about your looks?' Wayne asked. 'I'd think you'd care.'

'Why?'

'Your mother cares.'

'I am not my mother.'

On Wayne's bright cranberry office couch, I pressed my bare feet into the cracks between cushions. I lay back, turned sideways, placed my hands under my head the way I had seen a girl do on a train once, in a sleeper car on our way through Germany.

Wayne sat beside me, gingerly, and touched my hot head.

'Hello, Wayne.'

'Hello. Let's get you some dinner.'

'I'm meeting Ray.'

'You should be out with your friends, with people your own age.'

'It's good for us.'

'What is good for you?'

'It's good for me and Ray to spend time together.'

⚶

Maybe it was strange, as Keats says, for me to have let Ray into my life. Or maybe I thought that every good moment I spent with Ray could somehow cancel out the bad, could change my luck.

⚶

We walked into my room and the door closed, and the space under the door, too, when Raymond pressed a towel against it. He closed the window and the airshaft smelled of dirt and stale rain. I sat at the table, shrugging off my jacket and my scarf. He lit a cigarette, going back to the towel against the front door, squatting down and pressing the white cloth between the wood floor and the metal door, squinting to avoid his own cigarette smoke, which went upwards.

I fell in love with it. Not the way I fell in love with Frank, or even Beck, not for the rush of it, or the energy or the sky-on-fire way of it, but for the opposite: for the quiet of it, the focus, the hand that closed around my wrist and kept me still.

Lack of want—that is what I fell in love with, Ray and I sitting together on a bed, desireless.

⚶

There was Julep, Wayne's secretary. There was the medical director and researchers and visitors. I sat barefoot on the couch, door open or closed, during work or after, and Wayne didn't even think about it. It didn't even cross his mind, how we looked to others.

Good days, I had a vial of cocaine. Wayne and I went to *Le*

Balcon. I had wine so smooth and cool on the throat, when coke was rough.

'Don't you miss your wife?'

'Oh, yes.'

'Isn't it strange, not living together?'

He laughed. 'I suppose it is.'

'I wouldn't want to live apart from my husband, if I had one.'

'Oh, I suppose there's some deep dysfunction at the bottom of it. But actually, you might be surprised.'

'At what?'

'Well, she's moving.'

'She is?'

'We just bought a house. Do you want to see it?'

'You bought a house?'

'Small one. About an hour from here.'

'Mum never mentioned it.'

'She's got her feelings about it. Doesn't think it will work, I suppose. You want to see it?'

The garage had left his car in the sun. It was hot, the black dash soft like tar. Wayne listened to NPR and my eyes were sunken from sleeplessness. 'Can I smoke in the car?'

'No.' He always said no, but I always smoked anyway.

I rolled down the window and he pressed in the lighter for me. Once the cigarette was lit, he took it from me for a drag.

Then we were in Westchester, moving down the long quiet streets, turning into a loose gravel driveway and up to a gray wooden house, the roof slate and the trim on the windows white. Behind it were blue spruce trees and a swimming pool covered with a black tarpaulin.

'What do you think?'

'It's a house.'

'That's the idea.'

He stood with his back to me in his blue shirt. My chest hurt, right in the middle.

'Is she really moving?'

'Sometime. We just don't know when.'

I put my hand on a deck chair, iron and painted white.

'What's wrong?'

Everything would change, if Ida came.

'Come on,' Wayne said, crossing the grass. Inside the house, the carpet was white and the walls blue. The fireplace had a white marble mantel. In the fridge was a packet of crackers and a wine bottle with the cork pushed into it.

'Let me use the bathroom?'

When I came back, Wayne was at the kitchen counter, on a white barstool. 'Here,' he said, pushing my wine to me. 'How's Ray?'

'All right.'

'I'm not supposed to ask, right?'

'It's all right.'

'People have asked about you. People in the lab.'

'They have?'

'You're always late. You look exhausted. Your hands shake.' Outside, it was almost dark. 'What's going on, Betsy?'

I shrugged.

'Don't be coy.' He couldn't understand. How could he? 'What is it?' he asked.

'The thing is,' I said, and pressed down the base of my glass, 'I am the kind of person who falls in love with Frank, instead of Henry.'

'You can change that.'

'They always wanted me to get along with Raymond.'

'Forget Raymond.'

'I can't.'

'You look like hell.'

I shrugged.

He filled my glass. 'I am your friend, Betsy. You can talk to me.'

I smiled. '*There is a friend that sticketh closer than a brother.*'

'Are you doing cocaine? Is that it?'

'You won't tell my parents?'

'I swear.' He held up his hand, as if vowing. 'Not heroin, though?'

'No.'

'Can't you stop? For me?'

He wasn't my boyfriend. He wasn't my father or my keeper. 'Wayne,' I said, as if this was absurd.

'Just try. Just cut down.'

Dr. Keats thinks that Wayne's fixating on me was a way of compensating for not working on his marriage. He was trying to alleviate his guilt, Keats says, by helping me. I didn't care. All I cared about was that Wayne noticed me, Wayne cared for me, Wayne walked me across the white plaza after work, all the way to meet Raymond.

At dawn, smoke hung near the mottled ceiling. Smoke was killing the plants, I told Ray. One day they were green and the next they had dried up and blackened. 'Did you know that Wayne has a new house?'

'I didn't.'

'He does.'

'You've seen it?'

'Briefly.'

'Where?'

'Scarsdale.'

'Why did he take you there?'

'We went for a drive.'

'To Scarsdale?'

'Yes. Is that okay?'

'If you think so.'

'It's odd,' Wayne said, on the plaza waiting for Raymond, when it started to rain.

'What's odd?'

'It's like you're in thrall to him.'

'To who?'

'To Raymond. As if he has some power over you.'

His white shirt was showing the rain. The marble slab was shiny and slick. 'What do you care?'

'Betsy—'

'You shouldn't bother yourself.' I said that, but at least he asked. At least he wanted to know.

Ray was late. The air felt balmy, heavy and hot.

'Can't you stop?'

I took his hand, half holding and half patting it. 'You're so nice.'

'Bullshit. You're not seeing him tonight.'

'Wayne—'

'Get in the car.'

I didn't want to. If I didn't see Ray I'd have to rely on about one quarter gram of cocaine. 'I don't want to.'

'Get in.'

I got in.

The windshield swept the water aside. The roads were drenched and the trees dark. Wayne swung into his driveway, and the house was cold inside, a house hardly lived in. I did the last of my cocaine in the guestroom, sitting on the single bed with its white bedspread. When I came out, he had made us an omelet. He poured me a white wine and we sat on the floor, on his thick blue carpet, our white china plates on the glass coffee table.

Afterwards, he smoked a cigarette. I sat cross-legged in front of him, holding my wineglass.

'I wish you were my boyfriend.'

'Me?'

'You're nice.'

'You're nice, too.'

'Not always.'

'When were you not?'

'I wasn't so nice to Beck.'

'He wasn't right for you. Everyone knew that.'

'Is Ida right for you?'

'She's my wife.'

'I know.'

'There's Marcus, too. He's a great kid.' He trimmed the ashes on his cigarette, spinning it gently in an ashtray.

'If Frank drove up outside, right now, I'd probably go with him.'

'You don't know that.'

Yes, I did.

'You have to stop this business with Ray.'

'Okay, Wayne.'

I was depressing him. His shoulders were down.

He got up, suddenly, picking up his plate and his glass. 'Come on,' he said, 'Time for bed.'

In the guestroom, I could hear the wind in the trees. The slats of the blinds were open and outside was a great darkness. I got up and knocked on his door and sat on the end of his bed, crying, so he sat up, his knees raised and the sheets and covers pulled up. He was wearing a T-shirt.

'You have to help me.'

The cool even light of the suburban moon came through the windows. 'How?'

'I don't know. I just—'

'You just what?'

'Things are out of hand.'

'I can see that.'

'Although that is what I want.'

'Maybe it isn't.'

'No.'

'What do you want?'

I wanted to lie beside him. I wanted to stay in his room, room of blue walls and a blue duvet and black halogen lamps on the end tables. I wanted to start something new.

'I can talk to you.'

'So talk.' I lay back beside him.

'Be careful,' he warned as my body touched his.

Be careful? I almost laughed.

He pulled me beside him, his knees touching the back of

mine, and we slept, we slept all night. We slept until six-thirty, birds singing in the blue trees, and then I stretched my back, the way I knew I shouldn't. I moved Wayne's hand to my hip and then turned to him, lay my chest on his and kissed his mouth.

'No,' he said, but he was erect. I felt my eyelids tremble, like my hands sometimes, a kind of quivering.

He looked shy afterwards. He brought me orange juice and a fresh towel and later, driving to work, he worried he had taken advantage of me.

'Oh, Wayne,' I said. 'You did not.'

'You were upset.'

'You helped me.'

'But I can't help you. Not that way.'

Later I came to understand that nothing was ever final with Wayne; everything was changeable. Then I took him seriously, though, and I cried.

I cried in the car and I cried in his office. I cried on the phone talking to him from my apartment. Then I had Ray meet me where Wayne would see us. Wayne didn't like that, of course. *Meet me upstairs?'* he wrote in the note he dropped on my desk.

We drove to Westchester after work and the sun set on the thin young trees, girls stood on the sidewalk in their Dr. Scholl's sandals and tight shorts. We stopped at a market and Wayne cooked for me, Wayne fed me bread rolls with butter, ravioli with tomato sauce. 'You will eat,' he said, 'won't you? You will eat for me?'

Raymond started asking where I had gotten to, but of course I didn't tell him. I told him I needed a break for a while, so he shrugged, pretending he didn't care. At Wayne's one morning, I found his wedding album: Ida with straight chin-length brown hair, an ivory dress with a square neckline. My mother was standing beside her and Ida was no threat at all to her that I could see.

* * *

In the fall, red leaves coated the roads. Wayne drove to work early, and I walked to the train, along the quiet leafy well-painted homes, among American flags and SUVs that had nothing to do with me. Henry showed up at World Sight. It was my birthday, and he called from the lobby. He came up in his motorcycle jacket and cargo pants and boots, his hair pressed flat from his helmet, a silver cross around his neck. He had taken a year off college to research Christian evangelism on his motorcycle.

'Can you go to lunch?'

'Sure.'

I looked up and Wayne was at the door, hands in his trousers, slouching. 'Hey,' he said, raising his eyebrows, so I wanted to kiss him.

'Henry,' I said, 'Wayne Carter.'

Wayne stood up, stepping across the black linoleum floor to shake Henry's hand. 'The famous Henry.'

Henry grinned. He had just ridden all the way from a March for Jesus in Texas. I did some cocaine in the bathroom and we took sandwiches over to the East River.

'Your dad must really love what you're doing,' I said.

'He hates it,' Henry laughed.

'Is that why you're doing it?'

'Partly.'

'Do you even believe in all that stuff?'

'I like the phenomena. Like in Delaware—you drive down this highway and all of a sudden there's this statue of the Virgin Mary above you. Or you'll just see a cross suddenly, thrown up against a hillside. People have all this faith.'

'Do you?'

'I have faith that others have faith.'

Before he left that night, Henry brought four bags of groceries to my apartment. I felt bad watching him unpack—bread and pasta and eggs and cheese. I wouldn't eat any of that food.

'Have you spoken to Sylvia?' Henry asked.

'Not in a year or so.'

'She was asking me about you.'

He put a whole roasted chicken into my refrigerator, grease shining on the paper bag.

The phone rang. Raymond was in a bar on Ninth Avenue and wanted to come over. 'No,' I said. 'I'll meet you.'

'A date?' Henry asked when I hung up.

'My brother.'

'Eric?'

'Raymond.'

'*Raymond?* He's living here?'

'A few months now.'

'How is he?'

'All right.'

'Is he still on drugs?'

I waved my hand. 'Let's not talk about it.'

'Why not?'

'I just—I'd rather not right now. I have to meet him.'

'Okay,' he said, but he was annoyed. I couldn't blame him.

'I'll walk you out,' I said, and Henry got on his bike, an old Triumph, in his helmet and his cargo pants.

'Call me?' he asked, and I nodded.

I felt bad then—not because he was leaving but because I wanted him to.

Wayne called me at home. 'Let me come see you.'

'Now?'

I didn't want him in my apartment. It felt the way Ray's place had in Antigua, the one he and his girlfriend Alison had shared, all stuffy and smoky.

'So that was Henry?' Wayne asked, sitting at the table.

I had lit a candle. It was only a tea-light candle but I thought it might brighten the room.

'He seems like a bright guy.'

'He is.'

'Good-looking. Educated. What's wrong with him?'

'Nothing's wrong with him.'

'Here,' he said, pulling out a box from his raincoat. 'Happy birthday.' It was a gold bangle. 'It's not enough,' he added, slipping it over my wrist.

'It is.'

'Maybe by Christmas.'

'By Christmas what?'

'I want to help you.'

'I know.'

'I'm not helping you much this way.'

'You are.'

'I might have to leave Ida. I might have to face that.'

I never thought Wayne would leave Ida—not when he said he wanted to, not when he said I needed him to, not even when he said we would start our own life, somewhere new.

November passed, and most of December, and he listened to me; he bathed me and cooked for me and helped me to sleep. But he didn't leave Ida. He put his head in hands, right in front of me.

'You're ashamed,' I said.

'Well, Jesus, for Christ's sake, Betsy.'

'I don't want you to be ashamed of me.'

'I'm not ashamed of you. It's me.'

'Because you're with me.'

'Yes.' He looked tired.

I didn't want him to look tired. If he was tired he might stop seeing me. 'It's okay,' I said. 'Don't worry.'

He did worry, though. I could feel it. I went from him to Ray, Ray to him.

He didn't belong with Ida. Even my mother said that. The way he smiled when he saw me coming, the way he straightened up, against a wall in the hallway, at his desk on the sixth floor. He hadn't seen it coming. Not when I stretched out on his couch, not when he walked me across the plaza. But now it had come. Now, when he held me in his bed in Scarsdale, in the early morning, lying behind me, it had come and I could feel it, he could feel it, like something dark inside me.

Instead of leaving Ida by Christmas, he flew to see her. *This is the way of an adulteress: She eats, and wipes her mouth, and says, 'I have done no wrong.'* Ray came out of my bathroom and sat next to me on the bed.

'Are you all right?' he asked, thickly.

'I want to do it the way you do it.'

'No, you don't.'

'I do.'

He shook his head. 'I can't do that.'

'Why not?'

He sat with his eyes closed. His eyelids were dark.

'I want to, Ray.'

'No.'

'You're not making me. I'm asking you.'

He prepared the needle, the spoon, the brown powder turning liquid. He took the belt from my corduroys and wrapped it around my arm, a tourniquet. The syringe was orange and clear plastic. Once he got the needle in position, his hand shook.

'Oh, no,' he said. 'I can't.'

He missed my vein, a drop of blood bubbling to the surface of my skin. Sweat broke out on his forehead. Then he hit. I threw up into the toilet, the way he said I would. Then I sat back, my head against the bathroom tiles.

On Christmas Day, we were in Ray's old room at the top of the house, the same threadbare blue carpet, his blinds drawn and both of us sitting by the bed.

'What are you doing?' Eric asked, on the landing when we came out.

He could tell. He could tell right away. We had come out of the room too early, and I wavered before him. I thought I might fall.

'Betsy?'

He saw what I had done and I saw this settle into him—the way my own image had once settled into Beck.

He looked sick.

'What were you doing?' he asked again, and his voice was not natural.

'Nothing.'

'Ray?' he asked.

'Nothing.'

He always saw: here and in Antigua, in the bay and the ocean.

He took me by my arm. 'Come on.' His voice was so certain. I loved certainty. 'You're going home.'

'Eric.'

He led me down the stairs, Ray following from behind. 'Is this your coat?' he asked in the foyer, picking it up and handing it to me.

'Yes.'

He put it on.

'She's fine,' Ray said.

Outside, 64th Street was dark, ice sticking in sheets to the car windows. A woman was walking a sheepdog. Ray had forgotten his coat and lit a cigarette, smoke and steam making a white cloud.

Eric hailed a cab, holding Ray back from me with one hand and putting me inside with another. He gave me money for the ride. 'Go home,' he said, 'Go home.'

Ray nodded to me over his shoulder, and I knew what the nod meant. It meant he was coming after, he would follow me.

'Don't come back, Betsy,' Eric said, and the pain of looking at him, the pain of what he did and didn't know, was itself a needle, long and thin into the chest.

In January, when Wayne came home, I told him it was no good. Nothing was going to change and I should face it; he should face it.

Ray and I stayed up all night, so late that I didn't make it to work the next day but slept until three and called Ray again. Outside, the sky was blue like a child's sweater, the air cool and clean. People were carrying coffees and grocery bags full of food.

'Raymond,' I said when I reached him. 'You have to help me.'

'Do I?'

Then silence fell between us, silence like the old silence between our old bedrooms: the silence that went on until one of us gave in.

* * *

Two days later, I went to Wayne's office and closed the door and he put his arms around me, he took me back.

In February, it snowed. Wayne's blue spruce trees were frozen, the snow icy. Inside there was only me, the hissing of the radiator, steam from the shower. Then came March, ice cracking in the trees, glittering in the sun. I went to the park and watched it disappear for a whole morning once, trickling down the blackened plane trees, into the sodden earth.

'What are we going to do?' Wayne asked.

I was wearing longsleeves now, the way Raymond did, to cover my track marks. Wayne's indecision had begun to wear on me—the way he called from Belgium, saying he was trying to talk to Ida, the way he came home and told me I could not rely on him.

I took his car and swung out onto the street. I called Raymond from the car phone and met him at my apartment.

'Things not going so well?'

We went out for heroin and coke. I lit a cigarette and drank some vodka. We sat in the dark, mostly. He ran a bath and I sat beside him on the tiles, his head back and his eyes closed, his chest thin, his collarbone and ribs showing, faint hair on his chest, under his arms.

Late in the afternoon, at the window looking at the river, I pushed up my shirtsleeve. 'Look,' I said to Wayne, and he turned in his chair, smiling his bemused affectionate smile at me. Then his affection drained away, like color.

'Did you hurt yourself?' he asked. 'Is that a bruise?' I let him look until he knew what it was, until he felt it. Then I pulled down my sleeve.

'I'm sorry,' I pulled back, as if I really meant this, and maybe I did, nerves suddenly rising in me, hair tingling on my arms. Then I left the room, smiling at Julep, who didn't smile back, making my way down to the lab heady with fear, my heart beating and halls smelling of heat, of ammonia and the dark river. I took my bag and headed into the elevator, outside onto the white marble plaza, where I heard footsteps behind me and Wayne's voice, suddenly, calling my name.

'Come here.' His voice was angry. His voice was almost bitter. 'I want to talk to you.'

We walked to the garage.

'I'm sorry,' I said. Though I wasn't sorry so much as afraid—of myself and of the past, of what I had done and of him leaving me.

'You're sorry?'

He pulled me to a pillar, pushing up my shirtsleeve and looking again at the skin in the crook of my arm.

'God. I am such a fool.'

I fastened my shirtsleeve button. Without him, there was nothing good.

'You could have AIDS. Ida could have AIDS.'

'No.'

'Are you a child? Are you out of your mind?'

'I don't have AIDS. I used my own needle.'

His mouth was scornful in a way I had never seen. 'Your own needle. Christ.'

'I'm sorry. I didn't share.

'You don't know what you did.'

⚶

I was seven or eight or perhaps nine years old. Let's just say, to be fair, even, moderate, that I was in the middle—that I was eight and he, Raymond, being six years older than me, was fourteen. Perhaps I was naïve, untutored, ill advised. But all I felt was a vague surprise, a curiosity, Raymond standing beside my bunk in the boat, pulling back my sheet.

My parents were in the foredeck, Eric in the cabin bunk. Raymond touched me the way a doctor might—clinically, coolly looking at me as if at a scratch, a bruise, a bite on the inside of the ankle. 'You need to keep clean in there,' he said, so quiet, so calm,

I don't recall saying anything to this, or doing anything. I only recall the sheet, the raised nightgown, his fingers as he touched me.

Then my father came back into the cabin and Raymond stepped away from the bunk.

'What are you doing?' my father asked.

'Nothing,' Raymond said, and nothing was the same again.

I felt the steam of the shower water soft on my bare chest. I felt the wind at my ankles and inside my skirt. I felt Raymond coming toward me, the way you feel the end of day. I closed my eyes in my bedroom, the sound of rain dripping from the pipes. I lay down beside the water, under the bamboo, in the boathouse.

'*I don't like spiders and snakes,*' Raymond sang, sidling along the side of the house, '*but that ain't what it takes to love me—*'

'I don't want to hurt you.' If he hurt me I would bleed.

How to say how much I hated him? How to say how much I hated myself, there in the dark waiting for him.

꙳

I went home and I thought Wayne would follow me, but he didn't. Instead, Ray called from across the street, at the telephone by the plastic buckets of cut flowers outside the Korean deli.

Everything comes out eventually—at three and four and five in the morning, shooting coke and heroin with your brother. I told Raymond about Wayne and he told me that Wayne and my mother had been sleeping together for years.

꙳

'Didn't you know?' Dr. Keats asks.

'No.'

'You never guessed?'

'Why would I?'

Raymond was six the year I was born, the same year Wayne buried his first wife and first flew to Antigua. Maybe it was then that Ray saw how easy it could be: Wayne dropping his hand surreptitiously from the thigh to the inside of the thigh.

My mother was not cold. My mother liked men. She was the great prize in town, at least for my father when he saw her, thirteen to his seventeen. And for Wayne at Pigeon Point, their bodies side by side in the noon sun, perspiration on the back of the neck. In the evenings, they took showers, waiting for Edward to come home, for the candles to be lit, fish to be seared, wine poured.

'But you don't know,' I said to Raymond. 'Not for certain.'

'I know.'

'Is it even our business?'

'I'm just saying what I saw.'

'But we're grown now.'

'They were grown then,' Ray said, cleaning his clear plastic syringe.

John McCaney stands outside Dining Hall—tall, blond, a tennis player from Wilton, Connecticut. He is here for cocaine. Also, he is on probation for 'womanizing.' Still, I let him talk to me, him with his arms crossed in his white polo shirt, his silver Rolex and buffed white fingernails. I stand in my white shorts on the curb by the lawn, pushing at the grass with my sneaker, taking a cigarette from his shirt pocket.

In August, a heat wave comes to Fairley. Kenneth drives me to the doctors' office in the Lincoln. Only two pounds to gain and I'll be off car restriction. I don't know why they act as if I'm going to race around the grounds like the anorexic girls do, but they cover their bases.

Keats is out of breath, his thin blue shirt damp. I sit in a skirt and T-shirt, in my beige sandals, flat with straps. I hate girls who wear high-heeled sandals—especially in mental hospitals.

As Keats cools down, he breaks into a sweat.

'Are you all right?' I ask.

'Yes.' He wipes his forehead with a white handkerchief. 'I can come back.'

'I don't want you to come back.'

I hardly know anything about Dr. Keats. I know he is married because he wears a wedding band. I know he is from Virginia, because he told me. I know he drives a glossy black compact car, that his first rounds are at seven a.m. and his last at six p.m., and that when he is stressed, he writes lists. The day he told me this—about his lists—I felt so far away from him, I could hardly stand it. He was so different from me: his healthy skin, his quiet voice.

'Let's talk about Raymond,' he says now.

'*Thy brother came with subtlety.* That Raymond?'

'Is that how you feel about him?'

'Pretty much.'

'Can you say it in your own words?'

'My own words.' On the grass is a yellow flower, small and in the shape of phlox.

Keats's hands shake when he drinks water from his Dixie cup. 'Are you on medication?' I ask.

He laughs. 'No.'

'It's okay if you are.'

'Thank you.'

'Beck was about Ray. Frank was about Ray. Probably Wayne was about Ray.'

'You're still holding on.'

'To whom?'

'To Raymond.'

'Not to Raymond,' I said.

'To the way you felt about him.'

'Do you know that poem by Anne Sexton, "Wanting to Die"? It's in the library.'

'Probably not.'

'*Since you ask, most days I cannot remember . . . Then the almost unnamable lust returns.*'

'Is that how you felt?'

'Pretty much.'

'You were in conflict.'

'About the lust.'

'About making promises to yourself—and then not keeping them.'

'Exactly.'

'Maybe that's what you need to work on.'

'Promises?'

'The way you put yourself in conflict.'

I smile, but I look away again—at the shimmering, burning trees in the heat wave. 'Do you know John McCaney?'

'Yes.'

I shake my head. 'It's sad.'

'What is?' Keats asks.

I don't tell him, though. He is smart enough to guess. He should guess if he knows me at all.

'Once,' I say, 'just before Ray came back from Antigua, I was in Central Park on a bench by Sheep's Meadow. I guess it was during the week, because cars were going through, and I saw a silver Mercedes, like Frank's car. I remember feeling sick, suddenly, that it wasn't over.'

'What wasn't? Frank?'

'Not just Frank—me, my wanting to be with Frank, or people like Frank. I started crying. It was like looking into the future and feeling sorry for yourself before anything has even happened. I went to my father. I told him I didn't want to come to the airport to meet Ray, I didn't want to go to dinner.'

'And what did he say?'

'He said, *Why?*'

⚜

Wayne didn't call me. I called him, from my bed, as Raymond stood at the stove. He wasn't there, though. Ray and I mixed cocaine and heroin, which is known as a speedball, and then it was three a.m. and then four and then five a.m. Then Wayne was at the door.

'It's me. Open up.'

Ray picked up our kit, cleaned off the table, and took everything into the bathroom.

I opened the door and stepped outside.

'Jesus Christ, Betsy.'

'Ray's here.'

'I can tell that.' He took hold of my wrist. 'Come on,' he pulled at me. 'We're leaving.'

'We're *what?*'

'I told Ida.'

Some hopes you don't let yourself feel.

'You did?'

'Yes. We need to leave, right now.'

He didn't look so good.

'Okay. Hold on.'

I made him wait in the hallway. I made Ray give me a vial of cocaine. Wayne took my hand and I followed him down to his car. It was raining, a hard heavy rain.

'You look terrible,' he said.

'I'm sorry.'

'We need a few days. *I* need a few days.' His car smelled of cigarettes. I opened the window as he pulled out onto Ninth Avenue. We went west, to a parkway where the blossom trees were heavy from the rain, tulips black and purple in the grass.

'Look at that,' I marveled.

'What?'

'The green.'

Wayne took my hand. 'We're going to go away,' he said, 'for a week or two.'

'All right.'

He took my hand. 'You're cold.'

'Could we stop at a gas station?'

'What for?'

'To use the bathroom.'

'You have drugs on you, don't you?'

'No.'

'Don't lie to me.'

'Okay.'

'Give them to me.'

'Wayne—'

He held out his hand. His face looked old and I felt sorry for him, suddenly. I gave him the vial and he slipped it in his pocket.

'It's all right. I'll get you something.'

In Scarsdale, we stopped on the main street. The sky was pale gray, no sun showing. He wrote me prescriptions for Valium and Librium. He gave me money and waited outside the pharmacy.

'I want us to go away. Can you go to Miami?'

'Miami?'

He was serious. I was glad he was. Still, it gave me a shiver, somehow, realizing it.

'We need to be alone.' He sounded resigned, as if this were an aftermath.

'All right.'

He booked us two seats for twelve-ten p.m.

'Are we running away?' I asked.

'No.'

'It feels like it.'

'We're starting over. We're also getting you off drugs.'

He talked like a father, like someone who had never even done drugs, which maybe he hadn't. 'We're also getting AIDS tests.'

He changed his shirt, white for white, and his gray slacks for a pair of jeans. He looked different in jeans, innocuous, his back bent.

'What's wrong?'

'Nothing.'

We had a suite on the ocean at the Bal Harbor Sheraton. We ordered up wine and Scotch and tuna steaks that we hardly touched. We couldn't sleep, either of us, opening the windows for the warm air, closing them to run the air conditioner. Wayne counted the ribs in my chest. He took his wedding band from his finger. 'What do I do with this?'

'I don't know.'

He put it in my hand. 'Throw it away, will you?'

I went to the bathroom, thinking I could flush it down the toilet. I couldn't do it, though. I opened the window and put the ring on the ledge, where he couldn't see it.

We went to the Bal Harbor mall and Wayne bought me a bathing suit, sandals, pants and T-shirts and dresses.

'What will my parents say?'

'We'll deal with that.'

But we never did, deal with that.

I left a message for Raymond that I was in Miami. Then I didn't care anymore—about anything but Wayne. 'You're really doing it?' I asked, touching the side of his mouth.

'I am.'

He couldn't sleep. I woke in the night and he was staring at the ceiling. 'Wayne,' I touched his shoulder. But he didn't want to talk. He didn't want to make love either.

'It will be bad.' He looked at the drawn blinds. 'For a while. It will take a lot for both of us to do this.'

'You don't have to.'

'I know.'

'You're sure?'

'Yes.' He finally turned to look at me. 'I'm sure.'

I started to cry then, not from sadness or grief or even fear— but from relief, because I believed him. Wayne gave me another Valium and took one himself, so he could sleep.

It didn't help much. I kept opening my eyes to see him nursing his Scotch, looking at me or at the low lying clouds beginning to lighten in the dawn, the sun coming up in a bright pink ball. Wayne liked to walk in the mornings, on the beach when it was quiet. I watched him swim, his head bobbing down the shoreline. I watched him walk back to me, shaking water from his hair.

We had breakfast outside: eggs and bacon and potatoes, or sometimes just coffee and cigarettes, coffee and cantaloupe, coffee and Wayne's silence. We took cabs to South Beach and Miami

Beach, and back to Bal Harbor. 'You will marry me, won't you?' Wayne said, standing on the beach.

'If you leave Ida.'

'I have left Ida.'

Afternoons, we lay inside on the air-conditioned sheets. We started drinking and Wayne said we needed to make a plan.

'About Ida?'

'About us.'

I rolled off his chest, sipping from a glass of wine. 'You know,' I said, as the ocean rose and fell, 'Ray told me about you and my mother.'

'That was a long time ago.'

'Ray couldn't understand how Dad let you in the house.'

'Betsy.'

'What?'

He settled his eyes on me. 'Are you with me to get back at your parents?'

'Of course not.'

'Are you sure?'

'Of course I am.'

'That's what it sounds like.'

'How do I know that's not what you're doing?' I asked. 'Running off with me to get back at them.'

'Because I'm not.'

'Well then.'

'But you're asking me for answers.'

'I'm just telling you that Raymond didn't understand why Dad—you know—let you in the house.'

'Don't make trouble.'

I laughed.

'That's what you're doing.'

He kissed the side of my mouth.

'Am I?' I asked, kissing him back.

'Yes.'

'I'm sorry.'

* * *

It was AIDS or it was Ida, but he couldn't make love. Once, early in the morning, he woke and pulled me onto him. Even then, he stopped suddenly.

'What will you do,' I asked one afternoon, 'if I do go to medical school?'

Wayne smiled and took my hands, both of us naked on the bed. '*When* you go to medical school, I'll hang out my shingle.'

'Really?'

'Yes.'

'Wherever you went, you could do that?'

'Pretty much.'

'In Maryland?'

'Yes.'

'New Hampshire?'

'Probably.'

'Connecticut?'

He nodded.

I hate Connecticut.

⸙

They give shock treatments at Fairley, though not to me. Shock makes you forget. Mary gets shock and she forgets everything. She is an English teacher, but she can't remember what she has read. She carries a notepad so she can write down what happens to her.

Most of the books around here aren't so good, anyway: just abandoned crime novels, mysteries, and field guides to New England trees and flowers. In Dobson House, though, I found *The Crack-Up* by F. Scott Fitzgerald. It didn't seem like the kind of book they should have around here at all. But I read it, and it was really good.

⸙

The phone rang on the fifth day. It rang at six a.m., and at six-thirty as we left our room. 'Don't answer it,' Wayne said. He should have, though, I thought. He should have just answered it.

'Why not?"

He pulled the door shut behind us.

'What did you tell Ray?' he asked, as we walked to the ocean.

'Just that I was in Miami.'

'With me?'

'No.'

The sand was damp near the shore. 'Your father knows where I stay down here.'

'You think he'd call?'

'Him or your mother.'

We stayed on the beach until noon, until the sand was blistering white, the ocean pale blue and green. Wayne watched me walk to the water, my knees and elbows and limbs all sharp. As I swam, he lit a cigarette, sitting cross-legged in his new trunks, not as skinny as I was, but lean, long, with beautiful hands and feet. I came back and lay beside him, dropping my cold wet hand on his hot forearm.

'You're worried,' I said.

'A little.'

I wished he had answered the phone.

Down the beach, a group of high school students came down to the water.

'Because of the phone call?'

'Yes. Also the AIDS.'

'We didn't share.'

'Betsy—'

'Why didn't you answer the phone?'

'We need time, that's all.'

'Have you changed your mind?'

'No.'

He wouldn't look at me, though. I sat up and combed my hair and he still didn't look at me.

Back at the hotel, we took showers. Wayne was on the bed, wrapped in a towel from the waist, when the phone rang again.

'Betsy,' my mother said when I picked up.

'Mum.'

Her voice was level, not angry or cold or too warm. 'What are you doing?'

'Not much.'

'Is Wayne there?'

'Wayne?' He shook his head at me. 'No.'

She paused then. 'Are you all right?'

'I'm fine.'

The silence sounded like swimming, like the silence under water.

'You're sure?'

'Yes.'

Wayne had his head in his hands.

'Tell Wayne to call Ida.' My mother hung up.

I hung up. 'Mum says call Ida.'

His face was so white it hurt.

'Oh, God,' he said.

'Wayne.'

He started crying and put his head in his hands again.

'Wayne.'

'I'm so sorry.'

I sat beside him. I tried to touch him.

'Don't,' he said, and pushed me away.

I had known this would happen. Still I wished it wouldn't. Still I wished I could stop him, crying until he was sobbing, sobbing until his sobbing was a sound I would never get over. It was the kind of sobbing you do at a death—only worse, because I was not dead.

He got up from the bed, he seemed shocked by my presence. 'I've got to go out,' he said, and pulled his clothes on, went for the door. 'I'm so sorry—I just, I'll be back.'

I took the Valium and my clothes and three hundred-dollar bills. I left his ring in an envelope with his name written on it: *'Mr. Wayne Carter.'*

I didn't take enough for an air ticket, which I knew would bother him. But maybe that's why I did it. I shouldn't have made him suffer, maybe. But it was just a small suffering. For the first few blocks, I still imagined he might find me, might see me in the shirt and skirt he himself had bought me.

After an hour, I found a public phone booth with a *Yellow Pages* inside. I called up Drive-Away Services, which Henry had told me about. I took a cab to their office, about fifteen minutes north on a great rundown boulevard. They checked my license and I gave them $150 in cash, which I would get back when I delivered a new Lincoln SUV to Kansas City—a massive car, similar to the car Frank had—eighty-two miles on the gauge and four days to deliver it to Kansas City. After that, I was on my own.

Highway 95 was the easiest, air-conditioning at high, radio on. For some hours, I put the car on cruise control. I stopped for soda and cigarettes. I parked at night outside a Holiday Inn. I wanted to go in, but I didn't want to be in a room alone. The walls would be so white. The sheets would be so cold. In the Panhandle, I bought a boiled egg and an apple, which the counter man halved and wrapped in cellophane. At night, I turned off into a rest area and took two Valium.

By then, if he had flown, Wayne could already be home. I put the radio on and took another Valium and it was cold in the car. I was afraid to run the heat; I was afraid to drain the battery. I woke at three-thirty a.m. thinking someone was trying to steal my hubcaps. Then it was five-thirty a.m. and then six-thirty.

In Biloxi, Mississippi I bought coffee and cubes of caramel in clear plastic wrapping. I bought postcards of rundown hotels by the careless sea.

> *Dear Eric,*
>
> *Here I am in Biloxi. I have been in the sun and have a small tan. Hope you are having fun.*
>
> *Betsy*

* * *

Again that night I slept in the car in a rest area. I woke at seven-thirty a.m. to a truck driver warming his engine, combing his hair in his side-view mirror. I turned on the ignition to heat the car, and the man knocked at my window, wanted to know the time, he said. I shouldn't have let down my window. He asked where I was from and where I was going. He looked into the car and said it was new; it must have cost a lot; and how much was it?

I looked at him; I looked down and then away. I said yes, it was cold and so was I so I'd wind up my window and heat the car.

In Winona, Mississippi, at the Hitching Post restaurant, blue paint peeling from the shingles, a pink neon wagon wheel flickering on the wall, I ordered cereal and orange juice, eggs and white toast and grits. I didn't know whether to use salt or butter on the grits. I couldn't eat, so I left them plain.

In Arkansas, steam rose from the thermal pools. In Missouri, I slept on the side of the road, yellow fields in all directions. Then I was in Kansas. The Lincoln owner lived in a great new house in a great white suburb. He was balding, and looked like an engineer. His wife watched us from the kitchen window, and I would have liked a coffee, but they didn't offer me one.

'We asked for no smoking,' the man said.

'I'm sorry.'

A young man from Drive-Away Services picked me up. He was my age and eating a chocolate-covered ice cream. Back at the office, he gave me my $150. He dropped me at the Mission Inn where the light switch turned on both light and evangelical television station. I took a shower. I wrote a postcard to Henry, telling him this. I ordered room service but was too tired to eat. At midnight, Ray answered his phone.

'Hi,' I said.

'Betsy?'

I couldn't talk to him. 'Sorry,' I said and hung up.

* * *

It was hard to sleep. My room was on the street and I heard cars stopping. I heard people getting out of them and talking and then walking away. My bedspread was polyester and rough. It could burn me up, I thought, lighting a cigarette and then putting it out. Then I wept. I wept for a long time, not the way Wayne had exactly, not so a neighbor could hear me, but badly enough, badly enough.

In the morning, I had coffee and a donut in the lobby. I watched the local television. *'For thou are not a God that hath pleasure in wickedness; neither shall evil dwell with Thee'* (Psalm 5:4). I called a cab to take me to the Greyhound bus station. It was eighteen hours to New York City with a forty-minute layover in St. Louis.

The waiting area in St. Louis had a turnstile and security guard and chairs with built-in televisions. A kid across from me was smoking cigarettes and drinking root beer. He was about sixteen, I thought, and pretty. He had soft blond hair and ripped jeans and a diamond stud in one ear. He brought me a match for my cigarette. His name was Nick Johnson, he said, and he wasn't sixteen but nineteen. He was going home to Tennessee for his brother's wedding. Personally, he told me, he didn't believe in love. He had been in love once, but he had done something wrong and the girl wouldn't speak to him anymore; she told his friend he was an asshole. Since then, he had just been waiting.

I told him that waiting was good and not needing was best. It was when you needed someone that you were in trouble—because no one could give you what you needed if you truly needed something. Hearing myself say this, I started to cry.

'Wow,' Nick said. 'You are depressed.'

I felt the corners of my mouth turn down when he said this.

'It's all right.' Nick patted my back as I wiped my eyes. 'Why don't you come with me? We can stay at my parents?'

I thought about it. I really did. We smoked a cigarette and I almost missed the bus for thinking about it.

At three a.m., Port Authority was lit like daytime. I walked home in the cold. My telephone had six messages, but I didn't listen to them. I took the last of my Valium and slept for sixteen hours.

When I woke, I called Raymond.

'Are you all right?' he asked.

'No.'

'People are looking for you.'

He arrived in his ratty white sweater. He made us tea with milk and said, 'Well, you look good.'

'Thanks.'

'You have a tan.'

'A little bit.'

'Do you have any money?'

'Maybe.'

I called the bank. I had $454. Raymond and I went to a cash machine and took out $400. We went west and it was the same as always: Jesus with his blue shirt, Raymond with his nervous eyes.

It had been awhile, so I got sicker than usual. I had to sit by the toilet, throwing up. Then I started weeping—not knowing where Wayne was.

Ray went out for cigarettes and to the dealer's and to the store. We shot up in the dark, in the light, in the bed. "Easy," he said when my body shook.

In the bathtub, the water was gray, our bodies white and flushed hot. Our mother called but I didn't pick up.

'Why Wayne?' Ray asked, his back against the wall, a beer bottle swinging from his fingers. His eyes were sunken. So were mine. I could feel it, tracing my eyelids with my fingers.

'Do I look like you?'

'I don't know.'

'Your pupils are so small. It looks evil.'

I went to the mirror. My eyes were milky, my pupils as small as Ray's. 'I do,' I said. 'I do look like you. Do you know what Beck said once?'

'What?'

'That he didn't want to fuck me up.'

'What did that mean?'

'Exactly.'

I sat back on the bed.

'He couldn't really fuck me up.'

Ray curled up on the pillows against the wall.

'Why not?'

'I think I was probably already fucked up.'

'Were you?'

'I think so.'

Ray's eyes went flat. 'By me?' he asked. He handed me his cigarette. He took out his syringe. 'Probably by me.'

He started looking for a vein.

'You didn't tell anyone, did you?' he asked.

'Sure.'

'Why?'

'Why shouldn't I?'

'Who did you tell?

'Friends. Wayne. Dad.'

'Dad?'

'Last year.'

'Jesus,' Raymond said. 'Jesus.' He closed his eyes.

'Raymond.'

He just made it to the kitchen sink before he started to retch.

'I should call someone,' I said.

'No.'

'An ambulance.'

'It'll pass.'

It did—or at least the retching did. Then he lay on the floor, sweating and trembling. His eyes were like Wayne's on Miami Beach—full of fear. I went for a washcloth, washed down his face, his arms and chest. The color came back into his face. 'What did he say?' Raymond asked.

'Who?'

'*Dad.*'

He looked like a child—a child I had never seen. I could have hurt him. It would have been easy.

'He said things like that happen a lot.'

He reached for his syringe.

'What are you doing?'

'Do you want some?'
I did.

By the third day, the air was dense with smoke. It was five a.m. and we were being poisoned, Raymond claimed; we had to get out. He wore his sunglasses. We stood on the street and it was almost raining, the air misty with yellow smoke from some pipe. My knees gave way, so Raymond had to prop me up. He took my arm and we crossed the street. 'Jesus,' Ray said. 'Breathe.'

My hair felt dirty. I combed it back with my fingers. Ray took my hand as we crossed the streets, one after another, all the way up to the park. We sat by the lake where a wind blew up. Raymond gave me his ratty sweater.

It was so early, hardly anyone was around. Wind scuffed up the lake water. Leaves swirled in the tree above us, the color of plums. I watched a wisp of a spider crawl from the grass to my forearm.

Ray took out his needle. It was just like with Beck, on the bench in Central Park, the sound of rushing leaves feeling like they were rushing in my chest: leaves and the tops of trees and the heads of flowers.

'Ready?'
'We have to stop this.'
'We have a little left.'
'No, I mean permanently.'

I lay on my back, the sky becoming yellow like a jaundiced eye.

'Do you want to?' Ray asked.
'Yes. Do you?'
'Not really.'

The spider was a tiny whorl, legs like dandelion. It was strange, not hating Ray. I was empty. I was clean.

PART V

DAD ROLLS HIS eyes at Dr. Keats. 'Let me tell you about Wayne,' he says, my mother sitting beside him in an off-white dress. 'Wayne is an infant. Wayne has always done exactly what Wayne wants. Wayne is like a charming child, although I must say his charm has started to wear thin.'

'At least he listens,' I say.

'From what I understand, that's not all he does.'

'Edward . . .' my mother says.

'He sleeps with my wife, and he sleeps with my daughter. I hardly think I need to say more.'

'But what is really underneath all this?' Dr. Keats asks. 'For Betsy?'

'You'd have to ask Betsy that,' Dad says.

'I think what is important is that Betsy felt that Wayne listened to her. Is that right, Betsy?'

'It's easy to listen when you can just walk away,' my mother says.

'Exactly,' my father says.

It's not right for me to make out like my parents didn't try to help me. Maybe it feels that way, but they did try. My mother started calling me about two months after Ray came home. She wanted to know why I hadn't been by the house in a while. She asked what Raymond and I had been doing together. It seemed to me, though, that she had no right to ask—not when she never had before. So I wasn't very nice to her. To be honest, I think I was probably pretty cold.

One Sunday, my father called me from the street. Ray and I had been up all night. We went to a café and my father smelled of the inside of a store, fresh and new, and I hadn't even showered; my hands shook, I couldn't even touch my lemon cake.

'What is wrong with you?' my father asked.

My arms ached. My hair felt greasy. 'You should know.'

He turned his palms up.

'You were there,' I said.

It was interesting, because I felt my mouth turn, the way Raymond's does sometimes, both sullen and threatening, at the same time.

'On the boat.' I knotted my hair behind my head. 'You saw.'

'Saw what, Betsy?'

'Me and Raymond.'

'Things happen, Betsy. Things happen all the time, to all of us.'

The icing on my lemon cake glistened in the sunlight. The corner of my mouth trembled.

'You're not the one we worry about, Betsy.'

'Why not?'

'You're a strong girl.'

He dropped me off at my building. I turned and watched him as he left. He had no clue what was going on with me.

Late in the summer, my mother invited me to dinner. Wayne was in Belgium and Raymond had disappeared. I had no cocaine and was exhausted, irritable, and weepy. I didn't have money for a token, so I walked through the park. It was late when I arrived and Mum and Dad were in the garden with a lawyer from Dad's office. His name was Bobby Wynn. He was twenty-six and from Greenwich, Connecticut. He had a certain kind of handsome yet nondescript face: small perfect features and short thick hair. His suit was expensive, his tie loosened, and his jacket on the back of his chair.

'This is Betsy,' Mum said, 'our lovely daughter.'

Bobby Wynn wiped his hand on his napkin. He stood up and shook my hand. He had a nice smile.

'Betsy works at World Sight and Hearing,' Dad said.

Bobby had never heard of World Sight, so Dad educated him,

my mother pouring me a glass of white wine, filling a bowl of pasta.

'She's supposed to be going to medical school,' my father said. 'But we can't get her to stop working.'

Bobby smiled like a young man who understands the enjoyment of working too much.

'You should come out to Greenwich some time,' he said to me, 'have a swim at the club.'

I missed Wayne so much right then, I felt sick.

'Thank you. That would be nice.'

He smiled at me, an encouraging smile, and I felt sorry for him, that he thought he might like me.

My parents were pleased because Bobby was a nice guy, a lawyer, and smart. I felt bad for them, imagining we could ever like each other. Still, when Bobby Wynn called the next week, when my mother and father both called to see if Bobby had called, I took a cab to Grand Central Station. I took my sunglasses and my bathing suit and a vial of cocaine. Bobby met me at the Greenwich train station. He was wearing khaki shorts and topsiders.

'Are you all right?' he asked.

I put on my sunglasses.

'It's just bright.'

He took my arm and laughed—a strange, awkward laugh.

He had a VW convertible, tan leather seats and a glossy black exterior. I pulled my hair into a ponytail and we drove between the dull trees and the flat, luminous sound. He showed me his parents' house, a sprawling white complex with a swimming pool. He told me who lived in which mansion and who had before them.

He lit a cigarette with the car's lighter.

'You know,' he said, 'your dad is a popular guy.' I felt better, seeing him smoke. 'He's got that sarcastic sense of humor.'

'I know.'

'My dad is a little less verbal. But then, my dad is a banker— not a trial lawyer.'

'Do you want to be a trial lawyer?'

Bobby laughed. 'No. I just want to be comfortable.'

He put on a pair of neon blue–tinted sunglasses. His arms were tan. The sun was warm on my skin and I rolled my head to the side and watched the sides of the roads, the shadows in the shaded lawns and thick trees.

The club grounds were lush with sprinkler water. The horizon was all golf course. Bobby's parents were on the first tee. Mr. Wynn was slim and wiry and wearing a red baseball cap. Mrs. Wynn had that recently peeled look: her skin moist and too pale. I slipped through the shuttered swinging doors of the ladies' changing room and did a little cocaine. When I came back, Bobby and I went to the pool. He had a burger and fries while I had an iced tea and melon balls.

'No wonder you're so thin,' Bobby said, as we lay on club towels on wooden deck chairs. 'You're not one of those girls who starves yourself, are you?'

'I don't think so.'

''Cause I know a lot of girls like that. I mean, most of them are born here, but I got the impression at your dad's that you were kind of normal, you know, that yours was this nice normal kind of family from the British colonies.'

'We're normal.'

'People get so screwed up in New York, don't you think? I mean, it's so crowded and dirty and hostile. People are rude. And the *homeless*.'

I finished my last melon ball.

'The homeless are bad.'

Bobby stretched out in the sun. His bathing suit was blue with a paisley print. He took a lip balm from his pocket: cherry vanilla. I picked up a *Newsweek* from a stand, pushed back my sunglasses, and looked at the sky.

'You'll hurt your eyes doing that,' Bobby said.

He was very abrupt. I asked if he had liked law school and he said, 'It was all right.' I asked if he liked the law firm and he said, 'Pretty much.'

We didn't have a single thing to talk about. He didn't interest me at all—or maybe I was just tired. He told me that last spring he and some friends had gone bare boating out of St. Thomas. They blew a sail and lost the grill over the transom and did everything but run the boat onto a reef.

'Can't you sail?' I asked.

'Yeah, I mean we could. But, you know, the boat was some fiberglass bleach bottle, not a catboat.' Bobby turned his face to the sun. 'Of course, now that I'm at Tripp Stanton, I don't have so much time for that.'

He flicked a tiny spider from his leg.

'We should go dancing sometimes, get a group together.'

That would never happen.

'Maybe,' I said.

I sat at the edge of the pool, my feet in the cool water and my shirt open. Bobby came running from behind me, taking a beautiful dive: long and shallow and graceful. A young couple at the far end had their arms around each other. She was wearing a huge diamond engagement ring. I hoped I never wore a ring that flashy, ever.

'Very nice,' I said to Bobby.

'Thanks,' he said. 'Harvard diving team, actually.'

He looked good in the pool. The sunlight and the chlorine brought out his eyes. He swam over to me and took hold of my ankles. 'Don't,' I warned him suddenly, when I saw he wanted to pull me in. I had my vial in my shirt pocket. 'Don't,' I said again, when he ignored me.

He wasn't going to stop. I could see it in his eyes, the way they lit up suddenly, from the challenge. Then I kicked him, meaning to splash him, but hitting him instead. 'Jesus,' he said, pulling back from me.

He got out of the pool and the young couple was staring. She had diamond stud earrings to match her ring—just like her mother, I bet.

Bobby went off and got us iced tea. When he came back, I was in a deck chair, smoking.

'I'm sorry.' I was too. I hadn't meant to kick him.

'You're a little edgy.'

'I know.'

'What is that?'

What is that? I couldn't stand people who asked, *What is that?* I shook my head. 'Nothing,' I said.

'How was it with Bobby?' my mother asked that night on the telephone. I felt terrible, letting her down. 'It was fun,' I said

'Do you think you'll see him again?'

She was so hopeful, I felt sick. 'I don't know, Mum,' I said, and she went quiet.

$\twoheadleftarrow$

LAURA

Dear Betsy,

I only wish you had come to me years ago and told me about Raymond. I can't understand why you didn't, nor why, even now, you keep so much from me. I know Doctor Keats says we shouldn't discuss these things too much between us, at least not now when the past is so upsetting to you, but I want you to know that I am on your side, if there are any sides to this. I don't know what Wayne told you about him and me— but it hardly matters, at least to me. What matters to me is you, that you get well again and come back to us.

$\twoheadleftarrow$

In a hospital, they say you 'recreate' your outside world. This is known as *Mapping* and means, for example, that if you have two friends and one enemy on the outside, you will make two friends and one enemy on the inside. Keats says I choose people who take the 'focus' off me—standouts like Sylvia in high school, who couldn't walk down the street without people staring at her, or Robbie, the art dealer from Long Island who plays guitar with me on the Dobson porch. When the nurses found out that Robbie had bought me a skirt in the gift shop, they complained; they said one of Robbie's ways of Mapping was to take care of people like me.

Then there is Jo—Jo who would be beautiful if she were well, but who is not well, who is twenty-eight and looks old: her body clumsy from meds, her face lined, and her hair the color of dull bark. We met in Main House, in the lounge. My blood pressure was too low, from my medication, and I was on the couch eating Saltines. Jo was at a table, mixing cans of cranberry and pineapple juice in a cup of crushed ice. She had such tremors, she held her cup with two hands. The red and yellow juice stained her mouth.

'What are you reading?' she asked.

'*The Crack-Up.*'

She lowered her cup, running her tongue around her mouth. 'Good book.'

There is only one question you should answer '*No*' to at Fairley. This question is, '*Do you ever hear voices?*' To hear voices means you are not just depressed, you are not just in trouble, or exhausted, you are here forever.

Jo doesn't mind this. Jo says, 'Yes.' Jo says, 'Yes, I hear voices and I am possessed.'

Dr. Keats says Jo is schizophrenic and that most schizophrenics stay that way. Before she became schizophrenic, she was an English major at Smith.

It was Jo who told me that I was starting my sentences at the end and my stories in the middle. Because of this, and other confusion, I am on Haldol. This is a drug for psychotics, though I am not psychotic, Dr. Keats says. I am 'scattered.'

I feel scattered; I feel scattered around and cast about.

Afternoons are slow. We have Art Therapy and Occupational and Rec. Alcoholics sneak off in couples into the woods. Depressives set up deck chairs and read books about trauma and abuse.

In the pool, I float around in a Christ-like position. Tara comes by in a cream-white bathing suit, padded like something from the

1950s. People say Tara's husband is in the mob because he visits her in a cream-colored limousine and doesn't get out. Also, Tara has a woman bodyguard and every day her room is filled with pink and white canna lilies.

'Dunhill?' she asks me, sitting on the pool's edge.

I am doing breaststroke.

She dips a toe in the pool. Her toe polish shines like a tiny red traffic light.

'You're swimming.'

'Yes.'

She is here for alcohol and cocaine and Fiorinal, a headache medicine. Or maybe she is just here because her husband wants her to be. That's what some people say.

Sammy comes in and calls out that Dr. Keats wants to see me in Dobson House. I wrap a towel around my waist and squeeze water from my hair. Keats is with Nurse Caroline at the nurses' station.

'You didn't tell me you fell over this morning,' Keats says. The living room is empty, green light falling through the trees onto a yellow couch set.

'I'm sorry. I forgot.'

Caroline puts her arm around my shoulder.

'How are you, sweetie?'

In Dobson House, when I was in a bad mood, she used to come up to my room with crushed ice and a can of diet soda, which underweight girls weren't allowed.

'How's the big house?' she asks, taking my blood pressure.

'It's okay.'

'Are your parents coming up again?'

Everyone asks about my parents, once they have met them.

'Maybe.'

'Eighty-sixty,' she tells Keats. 'The heat affects her.'

'I think we should try some Ritalin.'

I like being watched over. I like it that everything I say and do—every tiny piece of information about me—goes to Dr. Keats.

'Is that all?' I ask, dripping pool water onto the green carpet.

Keats takes my hands. My fingers are cool against his hot palms. I know everyone is supposed to fall in love with their doctor, but I know, too, that I am not everyone.

'No tremors?' he asks.

He is about 5'10", the same height as Beck and also Henry. 'No.'

He smiles. 'Good. No more swimming today.'

Tara is outside with her bodyguard. 'Here.' She hands me a carton of Dunhill blue. 'For you.'

We smoke in our deck chairs by the Rec. Porch. The Dunhills last a long time, like Ray's English cigarettes.

'Is your name really Tara?'

'Delores.'

John McCaney comes out of Rec. in a damp T-shirt. He wipes a towel across his face, which is wet from sweat. 'Ladies.' He pulls a chair over to us, sitting at our feet.

His limbs are long, covered in reddish blond hair. The sun is in his eyes so he squints.

'Isn't she pretty?' John asks Tara.

A rush goes through me, like a ray of sun.

'She is,' Tara says.

'The two most beautiful women,' he says, placing his hands on our ankles. 'And I'm sitting with them.'

In the gift shop, I buy my mother a pair of earrings. Actually, I charge them, because I don't have any money, but they are cornflower blue and she will like them. She is easy to buy for, because she likes anything feminine: soaps, bath salts, scarves. Once, on Mother's Day, I bought her three baby dolls and tied their hands together: one boy, one girl, and another boy. This made her cry, for some reason. I have only ever seen her cry a few times: in the hospital when I was ten, the day Raymond left for Antigua, then the last time, the day she brought me into Fairley. Nurse Caroline had unpacked my bag, giving my mother my perfume so I wouldn't drink it for the alcohol. The perfume was Fracas, Wayne's favorite. Wayne had given it to me—and maybe my mother guessed this. Or maybe she was just upset about leaving me at Fairley. At any rate, she started to cry with the Fracas bottle in her hand.

It has been two months since I wrote to Henry from the Mission Inn in Kansas. First, he sent me my photograph of the tulips. Now he sends me a postcard of the largest concrete Jesus in the United States. On the back is written:

> *Dear Elizabeth, Betsy, Liz, Liza, Beth, Bettina, Bets,*
> *'Count up for me those who have not yet come . . .*
> *Gather for me the scattered rain . . .*
> *Show me the picture of a voice;*
> *. . . Then I will explain to you the travail that you ask to*
> *understand.'*
> *Ecclesiasticus 5:36-37*

I hope Henry finishes his thesis. I hope he doesn't end up in a religious cult or Tibet.

Raymond writes to me care of my parents; my parents send his letter to Dr. Keats and Keats asks me if I want to read it in front of him. I don't, though. I take it up to my room and the windows are open and the lawn has just been cut and smells sweet.

Raymond's writing is terrible: long and loping. The card is a little corny—a photograph of a lake by moonlight, a small boat tied up at a dock.

> *Dear Betsy,*
> *Here I am in Montana. It is so beautiful sometimes I think I have died. I'm staying with some old friends in this tiny little town. You probably can't even find it on the map. I couldn't. Missing you and thinking of you every day,*
> *Raymond*

He doesn't mention where he was when the police picked me up. He doesn't even mention whether he knows I am in Fairley.

* * *

I take the card to Morning Group.

Everyone there—except me—has recently attempted suicide. Meg is twenty-nine and a cellist and stabbed herself in the stomach with a carving knife. When I first came to Group, she said I reminded her of her. It seemed to me that there was a big difference between what she did and my overdosing.

Gregory is seventy-one and tried to hang himself when his wife died. Robin is from Westchester and Judith is a Jehovah's Witness from the Midwest. Then there is Mary, the teacher who gets electric shock, and Jo. I show Raymond's card to everyone and Lindsey says this might be a good time for me to 'tell my story.'

I tell them about Raymond, of course: about Raymond and Beck and Frank and me, Raymond and Wayne and me, Raymond and Wayne and my mother and me. Afterwards, no one says anything. They are supposed to say things. They are supposed to sympathize and make me feel better. This is known as 'feedback' and is an important part of our 'program.'

Finally, Lindsey asks if anyone has anything to share with me. Jo looks at me with heavy eyes. Mary lays her head on her lap. Judith puts her hand on her chest with her twenty small buttons. She doesn't mean to offend me, she says, but why was I pleased to hear from Raymond?

'Why?'

Lindsey leans in, looking all concerned, the way she is paid to. 'I don't hate him,' I say.

'But why don't you hate him?' Meg asks.

'Well, *personally*, I didn't think we were encouraged to hate people in mental hospitals.'

The sun falls in patches on the floor.

'Perhaps what people are trying to say,' Lindsey tells me, speaking too slowly so it annoys me, 'is that you don't have to hate Raymond, but after everything that's happened, you might not want to let him get so close to you.'

'But that's the point,' I say. 'We're the same, he and I.'

'You are *not* the same,' Jo says.

'Yes, we are. We don't like it here.'

Everyone goes quiet then.

'You were a child,' Lindsey says finally.

That's what they always say.

'It was still me.'

They don't like hearing that. But it's true. I get up and wave at them all, and then I am out the door.

'Bad day?' Kenneth asks, opening the car door, and I don't even answer him.

'What did you expect them to say?' Keats asks, an hour later. 'On the one hand you present Raymond as the root of all your problems—'

'He *is* the root of all my problems.'

'On the other, you see him as a kindred spirit, a romantic figure.'

'*Romantic?* I don't think so.'

'You pass around a card from him as if it is good for you to hear from him.'

'You think it's not?'

Dr. Keats shakes his head. 'You go from one extreme to another, which is what Raymond does with you.'

Do I go from one extreme to another? I walk around the grounds, to the chapel that is always closed. I stand on the smooth marble steps and light one of Tara's Dunhills. It had been so nice when Raymond was a friend to me—when Raymond was, let's face it, a little more than a friend—opening doors, propping me up in the street, holding my hand as we wove through traffic. But wasn't that better than what we had before? Wasn't that better than hating him?

It was, Dr. Keats says later. 'It just wasn't real.'

I am bored—but worse, bored by myself and by Dr. Keats, who asks, 'What's going on?'—as if I know.

On the lawn, I am annoyed at Jo's incessant talk of God. I am annoyed that it is so hard to make a string bracelet, weaving together red and orange and yellow thread from Occupational Therapy.

In Art Therapy, we are drawing 'how we feel,' and Robin draws a picture that is all black, with one pinhole of light at the center. When she explains that this picture symbolizes her depression, I don't think too much of her. Frankly, I always thought that people in a psychiatric hospital would be a little more complex.

Keats says I have trouble saying no to men because I have low self-worth. I don't see it. I think I have inordinately high self-worth because I can get any man I want, at least for a while.

Sylvia's buttercup Mercedes gleams on the hot black tar. I watch her swing up to the doctors' office, step out of the car in a white cotton slip of a dress and beige wrap-around sandals. It has been more than a year since I have seen her and she looks more mature, as we said in high school, her blond hair pulled back in a braid.

'Jesus,' she says, looking at my jeans, my shirt and boots. 'It's ninety degrees.'

'I should change?'

'Yes, you should change.'

I take her up to Main House.

'Very nice,' she says. 'Colonial.'

I fetch us apple juice and ice, which we take to my room.

'What should I wear?' I ask.

'A skirt.'

When I was a child, we went to a park called Fairyland. It had a wooden carousel and gliding bars so you could fly through the air. They made cotton candy, the grass was thick dark green, and I really thought there were fairies there. I'm glad I never have to go back there, because now I'd know it was just a seedy park, with broken swings and strange people my mother didn't want us to associate with. Luckily, with Sylvia, it is not that way.

'How long have you been here?' she asks.

'Three months.'

We stop by the nurses' station to get my meds. On the porch, I want to introduce her to Jo, but Jo turns her head away.

* * *

In the car, Sylvia turns on the radio. 'That place gives me the creeps,' she says, as we swing out under the heavy trees.

'I'm sorry.'

'Doesn't it give you the creeps?'

Fairley doesn't give me the creeps at all. I love Fairley.

'Sometimes.'

'What happened to you, anyway?'

'I don't know exactly. A lot of things.'

'Henry said you were on drugs.'

'I guess I was.'

'Remember how we did coke in the basement of school?'

'Of course.'

'We were so terrified.'

In town, Sylvia takes me to a fancy restaurant named Louella's. We have endive salad, trout, and raspberry parfait. It is the kind of lunch you have after someone has died.

'Henry has kind of died,' Sylvia says. 'He is born again.'

'No.'

'Yes.'

'He told me he was just checking it out.'

'Not anymore. He has a girlfriend who is also born again.' Sylvia rolls her eyes. 'Her name is Jai.'

'Jai?'

'A *yogi* term. It means victory.'

I go to the bathroom to take my medication. When I come out, Sylvia has paid the bill. We walk down Main Street and sit under an elm tree. Sylvia is remarkably calm. We are both twenty-four and she is in her first year of graduate school, getting a master's in linguistics.

'*I didn't want any flowers,*' she said. 'But I guess you got the hospital.'

Her hair has come loose; she twists a strand in her fingers as she talks. 'Not to be mean, Betsy, but you slur your words, did you know that?'

'It's the medication.'

'Do you really need to be in Fairley?'

'I don't know.'

'Maybe you just need some friends.'

'That's possible.'

'But it's worse than that, right? What you have.'

'Yes.'

'What is it?'

I shrug. 'Drugs. Raymond.'

'Your brother Raymond?'

'Yes.'

'What happened with him?'

'It doesn't matter now.'

Sylvia nods and takes my word for this. She is like my mother. 'Don't let anyone pull you down.'

She doesn't get it at all: It wasn't Raymond who pulled me down, but me who pulled myself down.

It has been five years since I last saw Frank Ravell, one since Beck. If I could, I would ask them up here and we could walk the lawn, stand under the trees and by the creek beside Bishop House. Beck and I could make love the way we first did. Frank and I would stroll the grounds, him holding loosely to my fingertips.

'You're so contained,' John McCaney tells me. 'You're like a Jack-in-the-box, all shoved down.'

'I am not.'

He is being kicked out for sleeping with a girl in the Adolescent Unit. Still, it is delicious, his body skirting mine, the smell of cut grass and sweet hanging branches, his sly admiring smile. 'Look me in the eyes,' he says, and teaches me how to kiss this way, the blue glint of him up close.

Jo's parents come to visit, bringing her sneakers and underpants and packets of socks. Jo's eyes afterwards are dark and remote. We go to Sunday barbecue at Rec., and it is so quiet, you can hear the flare of a match on a cigarette, the sizzling of hamburger patties on the grill.

Jo lies back on the grass, her new sneakers red with orange stripes.

'*Am I not an apostle?*' she asks, staring at the blue sky. '*Am I not free? Have I not seen Jesus Christ Our Lord?*'

'I don't know. Have you?' I ask.

'I have.'

She lights a Marlboro and the flame burns yellow in her eyes. 'You know—'

'What?'

'That is the Bible I was quoting.'

'Why would a prophet end up in a mental hospital?'

'Where else would a prophet be?'

Eric stops in on his way to New York. He has been at drama school. We have Cornish hen and creamed spinach and chocolate mousse cake. I take him to the library and the pool, and he doesn't say one word about Raymond or Wayne or Mum and Dad. He says he has been reading Berthold Brecht.

'Did you talk to him about anyone?' Dr. Keats asks me afterwards.

'No.'

'Maybe he was afraid to upset you.'

'It was as if he was visiting me at school, not in a hospital. I don't know.' I shake my head. 'Maybe it's good. Maybe he just accepts me. He doesn't judge me.'

'Why would he judge you?'

'I don't know. He was there.'

'Where?'

'Everywhere. He saw us, when we were kids, and then later, doing drugs.'

'So he withdrew.'

'I guess he did.' I pause. 'I mean, it would be one thing if he had just seen me and Raymond. But he saw other things. He saw me at the dockyard, too, with other people. I wasn't like the other girls.'

'What does that mean?'

'People could tell—some people.'

'People like who?'

'Like this guy Andrew, in Antigua. He was seventeen. He

worked at the dockyard and he knew, just by looking at me.'

'Knew what?'

'That I would do things with him.'

'Did you?'

'Yes. We went down to the dockyard, which was just being rebuilt then, and he took me into one of the ruins, into a square room with a stone floor and nothing on the windows or the door. He, you know—'

'What?'

'It's embarrassing. He, you know, fingered me.' I laugh. 'That's what they called it.'

'That's not abnormal.'

'I was *nine.*'

'You feel you were promiscuous?'

'Not promiscuous. Just, you know, sexual. Too sexual.'

'You felt people could sense it?'

'They could. Beck was the only one who saw me like a girl, who thought I was good.'

'Didn't you say once that you were wicked?'

I laugh. 'Probably. But I'm not wicked, either. I'm just—I don't know—worse than that. Weak.'

'I don't know anyone who would say you are weak.'

'They don't know then.'

Mum writes. She says Raymond has come home and she knows being around him is difficult for me, so whatever I decide to do—whether to come back home or move to Halfway House—is up to me.

꙳

We sailed all the way around the island, my parents and Raymond and Eric and I. We swam to shore in the morning, pulling ourselves up the hillside, through the loblolly and lantana, to a plateau where the jaquina smelled like honeysuckle.

I was afraid of the sea, of its depths and its darkness. I was afraid of rivers, of their reeds and murkiness. I did like the rain—

the dusk becoming night and rain moving across the water like tiny silver fish, a hard sudden rain tapping on the sea as on a flat roof, on the canvas bimini top and the teak decks and the crow's nest, streaming down my hair and face and throat.

At home, I lay in my room at the back of the house, a small narrow room painted yellow, a small square window open on the trees. My father sat on the bed, water dripping from leaves as he read: *'Macavity, Macavity. There's no one like Macavity. There never was a cat of such deceitfulness and suavity.'*

Today in Session, my father says that he feels he is being manipulated. He doesn't see how he is supposed to have sympathy for me when I won't even say what Raymond did to me. I pull up my legs in my chair. I will never tell him.

Keats says I can go either to Halfway House in Arizona or to Fairley House down the street. Both have openings on the first of October.

When my parents leave, Keats tells me he won't be able to see me, even if I go to Fairley.

'You won't?'

'No.'

'Why not?'

'I won't be seeing outpatients, not after September.'

'Not anyone?'

'No.'

You'd think I'd have some pride. But I didn't.

'Not even me?'

'I'm sorry.'

'God,' I say.

'I know.'

'It's like Wayne—how I, you know, made all this effort for him.'

'And now you're getting well for me?'

'Is something wrong with that?'

'I'd like you to do it for yourself.'

'For myself?' I laugh. 'I should have died—in Central Park with Raymond.'

Keats glances at the door. 'I'm not supposed to tell you this.'

'What?'

'It's not official yet. But I am leaving Fairley.'

'You are?'

'In October. Most probably.'

'Where are you going?'

'To Virginia.'

'Virginia.'

'I think we work well together. We have a good connection, don't you think? There's a charge.'

There was a charge. He had admitted it.

'If I could see you, I would. But I can't, you see.'

I nod, but I want to leave the room. I do leave the room, and Keats lets me.

In August, Tara goes to Sardinia and the second wife of a famous young novelist checks in. Jo and I watch her on the sun deck, her body as thin as a finger. We go down to Rec., set up a table on the back porch, and play Scrabble.

Raymond sends me Pablo Neruda's *Twenty Love Poems and a Song of Despair*, Keats is on vacation, and Meg tries to hang herself.

When Keats comes back, he says he is sorry about Meg. I say Meg just shows you how wrong you can be.

'She was hard to predict,' Keats says.

'She was about to go home.'

'Yes.'

'At least she had her chance.'

'What do you mean?'

'I mean, some people never get a chance—to get well.'

'That's true,' Keats says.

'So, she had hers.' I sound like my father.

'You sound angry.'

'Do I?'

'Maybe because I was away?'

'Maybe because Meg hanged herself.'

'Yes.'

I hold up the book Raymond sent me. 'From Raymond.'

'Ah.'

'Ah.'

'How did that make you feel?'

'You're the doctor.'

'I can't read your mind.'

'Why does he do that? Why send me presents?'

He leans forward in his chair, putting the tips of his fingers together. 'It makes him feel better about himself.'

I don't care where I am going after Fairley, now I know that Keats is leaving.

'You should care.'

'Why? Because you say so?'

'Because you're worth it.'

I laugh. '*I'm worth it.* Isn't that an ad for hair dye?'

Keats laughs.

'*Can I even write to you?*' I ask. '*Or do I just never see you again?*'

'You can write.'

'I can?'

'I might not write back, but you can write.'

'*I can write, but you might not write back,*' I repeat. 'That's nice. That's really nice.'

I stand up and want to do something to him, to push at him or slap him or beg him for something. Instead, I take my hair clip, hot in my hand, and throw it at him.

Outside, it is perfectly still. I can feel rain in the air. The clouds are low and dark. I run down to Rec. where Jo is outside, fiddling with a new leather bracelet. We stand on the porch and watch the wind in the grass and trees. Lightning turns the sky electric white, the same white as Jo's teeth. She puts her hand on my shoulder. Her eyelashes are wet and her eyes wide like the eyes of a doll.

'It's beautiful,' she says.

'Yes.'

She takes my face in her hands. Her hands are rough, yet at the same time gentle.

'Don't, Jo.'

'Can I kiss you?'

I take her hands from my face. I can feel tremors in them, like currents in water.

'No.'

She starts to cry then and I can't stand it—her heavy body, her eyes so wide open and pained. I put my arms around her, around her thick dark hair smelling of grass and smoke.

'Just once?' she asks.

'Jo—'

I push her back by the shoulder. Her mouth trembles and she is going to keep crying, going to give in the way Wayne did, so I couldn't help him. 'Stop it,' I say, 'stop it stop it,' my voice like Frank's in his room in the dark. I slap her so hard she flinches. She steps backwards and knocks the Scrabble set from the table.

'Get away from me.'

She holds her hand to her cheek. But I didn't hurt her. There is no red mark.

'You don't have to stay here,' she says.

'Oh, no?'

'You can come with me.'

'To where?'

'To God.'

'To God?'

'It's not so hard.'

'Then why do you want to kiss me?'

'It's lonely sometimes. Being human.'

'You *are* human.'

'Only with you.'

She starts running, big and awkward in the rain across the grass. I pity her, but at the same time, I hate her. I hope I never see her again. She disappears into Bishop House and I go up to Main and the nurses are rushing about, slamming windows against the rain. I don't shut mine, though. I lie soaked on the bed, until the sky is almost black, until a cold breeze drifts in and my door opens.

I see Keats's shoes and trousers.

'Betsy?' His voice is gentle, almost sorry.

'Yes.'

Vicki comes in after him and starts to take my blood pressure.

'Jo has run away.'

'Has she?'

He turns on the lamp by the bed.

'Sammy says you were together at Rec.'

'So?'

'Did something happen?'

The room is shadowy and cold.

'Actually, I hit her.' Vicki raises her eyebrows at Keats. 'I saw that,' I tell her.

'Why did you hit her?' Keats asks.

I turn onto my side on the bed, my hands between my knees.

'Betsy.'

'What?'

'Sit up.'

I groan and stand up and walk over to the desk between the open windows.

'What happened?' Keats says again. The breeze is cool and strong.

'She asked me to kiss her.'

'And did you?'

'I'm not sure that's your business, really—are you?'

Keats comes toward me. His face is pale and smooth, darkness all around him. My arms ache. The insides of my elbows ache, as bones do, before rain.

'Sit down.'

'Why should I?'

'I'm here to help.'

'You're *leaving*.' I am too intense. No one likes this. I like it least.

'Not right now.'

'Soon enough.'

'Come on, Betsy.'

'You don't care about me. You care about Jo, maybe, because she's missing. And you care about her kissing me. But you don't care about me.'

'That's not true.'

'You want to know what happened—you and Vicki both. It's exciting to you.'

'You're just upset.'

Vicki leaves the room.

'Where did Jo go?' Keats asks me.

'I don't know.'

Vicki comes back with another cup of liquid Haldol. I let her walk right up to me, holding out the cup. Then I slap it away. I slap it so hard it hits the wall, liquid splashing Keats's shirt, sliding down the glossy blue painted wall.

'That's enough,' Keats decides.

'Oh, is it?'

'You need to calm down.'

I have an urge to slap him. I lift my hand, but he catches it.

'I hate you,' I say. 'Did you know that?'

He flinches. I have hurt him and I am half glad.

'You don't mean that.'

'I do.'

Though I don't, of course. Though I just cannot believe he would leave, how it will be, again, after this.

'Get a Special,' Keats tells Vicki.

Specials are for psychotics. Specials follow you everywhere, all the time.

'What?' I ask. 'Are you afraid of me?'

Wally comes in then, 6'1", 240 pounds, half Special and half Security. Lola from Jamaica follows him.

'Bastard,' I say to Keats as they hold me down and Vicki injects me.

PART VI

THE SKY IS misty when I wake. Ash gray light fills the spaces between leaves. I go down the hallway in my pale blue nightgown. Lola is my Special and follows me, her skin black and luminous in her white uniform and white knee socks. We sit on the paisley couch and she lights my cigarette for me, puts it out when I am done.

Later, I take a shower and Lola goes through my closet, picking out clothes for me to wear. I choose a pink skirt I just charged at the gift shop. Pink is not a color I usually wear, but I don't want to be like Robin with her all-black painting. Outside, it starts to rain and a nurse brings me my meds. Lola gets our breakfast and at seven a.m., Dr. Keats comes in.

'You're angry,' he says, and I don't answer. Or I can't, because who knows what I might say, what it could start. Still, I am glad he is not angry at me.

Kenneth drives me to Morning Group. Lola and Adam ride with me and Lola tries to sit me between them, like some unruly child. I wouldn't care, if it was just Lola. But Adam is my age, Adam is handsome, with his curly dark hair. 'Oh, for godsakes,' I say and lunge for the door. I open it so the air floods in, hot and humid, so the black tar road rushes beneath us. Lola pulls the door shut and Kenneth stops the car. Kenneth turns around and heads back to Main House.

They move me to a room off the nurses' station, so they can watch me better. It is a small dark room, a blue drape hanging over the window. Keats must be in session, because another doctor—Jo's doctor—comes to see me. Her name is Dr. Caroline Spiro and she is from Connecticut. Her hair is straight and blond like my mother's, only shorter. She is wearing a summer suit, like someone in corporate relations.

She has a Klonopan for me. I can see it inside a plastic cup.

'Why did you open the car door?' she asks.

'Is that for me?'

'Bring a cup of water,' Dr. Spiro tells Lola. She goes to the bathroom and we wait for her to come back. Then Spiro hands me the pill and the cup of water.

'Thank you,' I say, and swallow the pill. 'Frankly, I didn't think I needed *three* people to take me to Group.'

'That's what your doctor ordered.'

I shrug.

'This is a *psychiatric* hospital, Betsy.' She has an engagement ring in the shape of a pear. She looks like nothing bad has happened to her, ever. 'You can't go around opening moving car doors.'

'Oh.'

'I understand you were in Dobson House—'

'So?'

'Were you trying to get more drugs?'

'I'm sorry?' I say this the way we said it at Houghton, real sarcastic.

'It's not uncommon for people to create a disturbance in order to get more medication.'

'I'd like to see Dr. Keats.'

'I'm afraid he's busy.'

'You're Jo's doctor aren't you? Jo Whelan?'

'Yes.'

'She's not doing too well, is she?'

The bed is lumpy and damp and old smelling. Even the blanket is old smelling, wool and dark green. I have a feeling that someone has died here, perhaps recently. When Vicki comes by, I ask her about this. She can't remember anyone dying, though.

I lie in bed and then I fall asleep, the way I always do with Klonopan or Haldol. When I wake up, Dr. Keats has come. 'Feeling better?' he asks, pulling out the wooden desk chair.

I sit up on the bed. 'I was fine to begin with.'

'Come on,' he says. 'Let's talk in the nurses' station.'

Part of me wants to stay where we are, to have him sit in the chair beside my bed, to have us all alone. The other part is scared of this, as if I might say something I should not, as if my heart, which is full with him, might grow too big inside my chest.

We go to a desk by the blood pressure monitor. As usual with Keats, I am wide awake suddenly.

'So, you saw Dr. Spiro.'

'I did.'

'You didn't like her too much.'

'I'm sorry.'

'Why did you open the car door?'

Adam is on desk-duty, pretending to read a textbook.

'Hi, Adam,' I say, smiling at him so he actually blushes.

'Why did you open the car door?' Keats asks again.

'I don't know why.'

'You can do better than that.'

'Adam was there. Ask Adam.'

'Adam,' Keats says, 'would you give us a minute?'

'Sure.' He goes out of the room.

'He's cute,' I tell Keats.

'Is he?'

'I didn't mean to open it. I didn't plan it.'

'Did you plan to jump out?'

'I didn't really think about it.'

'You just can't do things like that.'

'I know—Dr. Spiro told me.'

'You scare people.'

I laugh. 'Do I?'

'You scared me, when I heard.'

I feel bad then. 'I'm sorry.'

'Can you try something for me?'

'What?'

'I'd like you to think back to the moment just before you opened the door. Can you remember what you were feeling?'

'I don't know. I was embarrassed.'

'Because?'

'Because, I don't know. Adam is my age. Lola was all over me.'

'That's her job.'

'It just—it was embarrassing.'

'So the next time you feel that way, I'd like you to stop for a minute, to try to identify what you're feeling, and then express yourself.'

'Express myself?'

'You don't express yourself. Not directly. You need to say what you feel when you feel it. Can you try that?'

I wince. I am not sure this technique will work.

'Pretend it's happening right now. Pretend we're in the car. What would you say to me?'

'I'd say, *Stop it. You're embarrassing me.*'

'Exactly.'

'But that's embarrassing, too. Just saying that would be embarrassing.'

'For you.'

'Yes.'

'Practice.'

They find Jo in the woods, in her bra and shorts, all scratched up and dirty. I want to see her, but Dr. Keats won't let me. 'You're talking about someone who came on to you sexually—someone who made you jump out of your skin.'

'Maybe that's what I need.'

'To jump out of your skin?'

'Maybe.'

'She crossed a line with you.'

'True.'

'It gave you a shock.'

'She is not well.'

'No, she isn't.'

'I like her, though.'

'I know you do.'

Keats stands with his smooth white hands on the back of the desk chair. I am on the armchair and between us is my bed.

'I'd like you to try to go to Group this morning.'

I don't want to go to Group. At the same time, I am bored.

'All right,' I say. He turns to leave. 'Dr. Keats?'

'Yes?'

'You said Jo gave me a shock—'

'Yes.'

'Well, they all do.'

'Who does?'

'Everyone: Beck, Frank, Wayne. They all give me a shock.'

'They're pretty shocking.'

Keats puts me back in my regular room, my big blue airy room overlooking the white birch trees.

In Stress Management, on the porch behind Rec., Sammy makes us write a list of things at Fairley that we like to do. I write:

1. *swim*
2. *smoke*
3. *sleep*
4. *look at trees*
5. *get mail*
6. *see Keats*

Meg used a sash to hang herself. Robin uses strips of a linden tree. She doesn't die, though. She is transferred to another hospital.

In Group, Mary is the most upset. She thought Robin should have warned her. She thought Robin trusted her.

'I guess you were wrong about that,' I say.

'Betsy,' Lindsey warns. I hate being warned. Warnings make me worse.

'I just don't really think people at Fairley should be trusting each other.'

'Mary is allowed to be upset.'

'Robin could have warned someone. She knew what she was going to do.'

'I think,' Judith says, in her buttoned-up blouse, 'that all of us here should realize that Robin is a sick child, a sick and very needy child. And there are powers greater than us that lead someone to do something so terrible.'

'Powers greater? What about powers smaller? What about being sick to death of it all. What about that?'

Judith rests her frail religious hand on her flat chest. Mary writes something on her ECT memory pad.

'I'm sorry,' I say, 'but I have to leave.'

'Betsy,' Lindsey says, but I don't go back.

Kenneth pushes off the car.

'They're getting to you, sweetie?'

Keats comes to my room in the afternoon. I sit in the armchair and he sits at my desk. 'So you left Group?'

'I did.'

'Because of Robin?'

'Robin?' I pretend to wonder who this is. 'Robin can go to hell.'

Then I feel evil. 'I'm sorry,' I say. 'I didn't mean that.'

'You're under stress.'

'I don't feel stressed.'

'You look stressed.'

'Do I?'

'Yes.' Not even the Klonopan is working. Klonopan takes my past and wraps it in a ball and rolls it away.

Outside the window, I can see the alcoholics coming up the lawn in a cloud of smoke.

'All this fuss about Robin—she's not even dead.'

'Is that why you're angry?'

'She was always complaining. Meg didn't complain.'

'But Meg is dead.'

'She is.'

'Are you angry that Robin didn't die and Meg did?'

'Well, Robin did want to.'

'And Meg didn't?'

'No more than anyone else.'

He looks at my pictures on the wall. I have one of Henry on

his motorcycle. I have one Beck sent me from the Marines. I have one of Keats, of course, and I hope he doesn't make too much of it.

'You identified with Meg.'

'Not particularly.'

'Didn't she tell you that you reminded her of herself?'

'That was months ago.'

'But she said it.'

'Yes.'

'And she surprised you.'

'Yes.'

'The way you surprise yourself.'

'I'm not going to kill myself, if that's what you're getting at.'

'But you're angry.'

'I know that—God.' I look out the window again, shaking my head.

'So what are you going to do about it?'

'Dr. Spiro seems to think I don't know how to behave in a mental institution.'

The cloud of smoke turns into three clouds as the alcoholics split up for their next groups.

'Forget Dr. Spiro.' He points at Henry's picture. 'Who is this?'

'Henry.'

'What's the worst that could happen, if you got angry?'

'I don't know. I could hit someone. I could hurt myself.'

'Have you thought about hurting yourself?'

'Of course.'

'Does anything come to mind?'

'Just running into the fucking road.'

'Can you see yourself doing that?'

'No,' I say, disappointed.

'You're not a mean person. Tell people you have a problem with anger. Tell them you're working on it and don't mean to hurt anyone's feelings.'

'Unless I do.'

'If you do, tell me. Or one of the nurses.'

'All right.'

'You think you can do that?'

'I can try.' I smile. He gets up to go. 'By the way—' I say.

'Yes?'

'That's your picture.'

'It's not very good.'

'Do you think I'm weird?'

'No. I'm flattered. We're friends, aren't we?'

'Yes.' He is about to leave. 'Oh, Dr. Keats?'

'Yes.'

'I wanted to tell you. The shelves in the bathroom cabinet are glass.'

'Are they?'

'You can lift them out, if you want to.'

'Thank you for telling me that.'

The next day, the shelves in my bathroom are changed from glass to plastic. I fall asleep by the pool and wake to Lola telling me I am late for Dr. Keats. I am enraged at this. I 'express' my anger to Lola. I express it again to Kenneth in the car, saying I know I am childish.

'You are what you are,' Kenneth says.

At lunch, Dr. Spiro is at the salad bar, tongs around an artichoke heart.

'Bitch,' I say under my breath.

She is good, though. She is as good as me.

'What was that?' She turns to me. 'Did you say something?'

'I don't think so.'

'Playing games again?'

I pick up a peach from a cobalt blue fruit bowl. It is a little overripe, and soft.

'You're not exactly a sympathetic doctor, are you?'

'I think you and I should talk, Betsy.'

'Right now?'

'Upstairs.'

'Not my doctor's orders.'

Spiro calls for Adam. 'Take Betsy to the nurses' station.'

'God,' I say again. 'Really.' I take my peach and throw it at her. It misses her and hits the blue wallpapered wall behind her with a thud.

'Betsy,' Keats says, back in my room again, me all drugged up on Haldol.

'What?'

'What are you doing, picking a fight with Dr. Spiro?'

He goes to the bathroom and brings me a glass of water.

'You're ignoring the truth,' I say.

'Which is?'

'I was there. I was there. I was there.'

'Where?'

'With Raymond. I wanted him to touch me.'

'You were a girl.'

'I've heard that theory. I was a girl, so it wasn't my fault.'

'It's hard enough for adults.'

'It doesn't make any difference.'

'You have to stop.'

'Stop what?'

'Punishing yourself.'

'Punishing myself?' I laugh. 'I am not punishing myself.'

'What are you doing then?'

'Living with myself. Living with the truth of myself.'

'Which is?'

'That I could never say no. That I can't trust myself. That I disgust myself.'

'That's not punishing yourself?'

'No. Did you see the peach?' I ask, smiling, so he smiles back.

'Everyone saw the peach.'

'You know what punishing yourself is? Punishing yourself is hating someone and then letting them touch you. Do you know what that's like?'

'I'm not sure I do.'

'Have you ever done it?'

'I've been angry at people—and then gotten over it.'

'But what if you didn't get over it? What if you hated someone and still let them touch you? What about that?'

'It sounds painful.'

'It is.'

'I think you can change.'

'Do you?'

'If you want to.'

I would like to believe him. I would, but it doesn't seem likely.

Even though I have just thrown a peach at Dr. Spiro, I am supposed to be planning my 'Aftercare.' This is because my insurance is running out. Keats and I take a walk around the grounds, and the lawns are still green with sprinkler water, the chapel is still closed. We stop on the white marble steps and it is hot. I light a cigarette, and Dr. Keats shields his eyes from the sun.

'I could get a job,' I offer.

'I don't think you're ready for that.'

'I could go to New Haven and stay with Eric.'

I put out my cigarette in a strategically placed bucket of sand.

'No,' he says.

'No?'

I like it that he tells me what to do.

Back in his office, I swing my foot in its low black sandal.

'I am just the same.'

'No, you're not.'

'How am I different?'

'You're angry.'

'I've always been angry. So they say.'

'Not openly.'

'Maybe.'

'It's a step.'

'Maybe I could move to Virginia.'

'To Virginia?'

'Yes.'

'To follow me?'

'Is that so bad?'

'You'd base your life on our relationship?'

He is mocking me; the idea is ridiculous to him. I feel my body recoil as if in a trap. 'Oh,' I say. 'That was mean.'

Now he pities me. I feel sick at this. I have to leave or it could get worse. I remember Wayne sobbing in the hotel. This is not the kind of thing I want to hear, feel, or see again.

'What are you doing?' he asks.

I shake my head. 'I've got to go.'

'Session isn't over,' he says.

'It is now.'

I push open the glossy white door. The parking lot glimmers with its glass asphalt. He is following me and will make things worse. 'You should leave me alone. You should start *now*.'

'Betsy.'

I am walking fast, and he fast beside me. I turn right, past the library and up to the Main House porch. I take the stairs to the first landing where the window is open and a breeze passes through the room.

It smells like summer, with all the flowers dried up. I stop near the window. Keats stands with his feet apart, pressing his fingers together.

'People come along,' I say. 'They try to help. They show you that they could help, that it is possible. But then in the end, they can't help. So it makes it worse. You get your hopes up. They should have just stayed away, in the first place. I mean—why bother? Why did Wayne bother? Why torment me?'

'Sit down, Betsy.'

The lawn is yellow with late sun. 'Look at that,' I say, gesturing.

'What?'

'It's beautiful out. I do nothing but sit here talking about myself.'

'You are in a psychiatric hospital.'

'Nothing lasts.'

'Betsy.'

'Nothing lasts. Though, also, nothing changes. It's incredible.'

'Betsy.'

'I am tired of this. I thought I could change. This is my last attempt. But I can't, you see. I can't. I can't. I want to get out.'

'Out of what?'

'Out of my life. It's just the same thing, over and over. It's too much. It's not like I haven't been trying. I have tried. I tried with Beck and Frank and Henry and all the others. I tried with Ray. I tried to stop myself, to change myself, to feel like someone else. I wanted to die, in my room with Ray, in Miami after Wayne. But it just goes on. It's amazing. It gets worse.'

I am crying now. My face is wet with tears. Lola brings me tissues but I push them away.

'Wait here,' Keats says.

'What, are you going to get more drugs? So you can calm me down, prolong it all for me?'

'Stay there.'

I curl up in the armchair. Lola sits on the armrest. Then Wally comes in, dressed in black with high-top sneakers.

'What are you doing?' My bitterness hurts me.

'Watching you.'

'Lola's watching me.'

'Doctor's orders.'

'You like this, don't you?' I ask them both. 'You like seeing people in distress.'

I don't want any more meds. I don't even want Keats. I am out the door and down the stairs before Wally can catch me. I am on the lawn and down the hill, Wally calling my name, calling, 'Stop it, stop it, stop.'

There is nowhere to go, really, unless I go on the road. But I don't go on the road. I spin around, suddenly, in the sweet lawn, near the high trees.

'Why?'

'Because, Betsy. They'll put you in Little House.'

Little House, where the suicides are, psychotic Paula and David in restraints.

Keats comes over the hill, in his khaki pants and blue shirt. Lola waits at the top, her white uniform like a flag.

'Hello, doctor,' I say, when he finally reaches me.

'That's enough.'

'Is it?'

His shirt is damp with sweat. This is because of me, because he came running for me.

'I'm putting you in Little House.'

I smile. 'Oh, come on,' I say, looking off at the shimmering black tennis court.

He has a plastic cup in his hand. 'You're upset.'

'*Upset.* Why don't you say what you really think?'

'Which is?'

'You're not my friend. You won't even see me again.'

He looks at his hands. The plastic cup has buckled in the middle. 'Drink,' he says, so I take the cup—clear warm Haldol swimming like hope—and I tip it out, ever so slowly, into the lush grass.

Little House is at the foot of the hill, to the left of Bishop, small and rectangular like a classroom or a cabin painted white. They give me so much Haldol, I am heavy with it, cloudy and dense.

At the same time, I am hot, in a fever and on fire. Lola takes me from the bed, her black hand around my skinny arm, both wet from my sweat. She leads me to the white shower, takes off my blue nightgown, sets me in the streaming tepid sheets of water, the soap slippery in my hands so I drop it in the tub, watch it swim in a puddle near the drain.

'Sweetie,' Lola says.

Or maybe she doesn't.

Sweetie

Honey

Darling

Miss Scott

I will never have a good life.

* * *

From my bed, I see the nurses come and go. My head hurts from weeping. My sheets make a tangle on the floor. 'Don't,' a male nurse tells me, sitting in the corner in the hardback chair, as I cover my face. 'I want to see you.'

I dream of green water, of standing in it, up to my waist in the light green dazzling light and silky weight of it. The sky is shocking blue. The sun is coming in shards. I have my arms around a man. I see his face and then it changes. It is Beck and then Frank and then Andrew and then Wayne. It is all the men I have known, one after another, in my arms.

Last to come is Jesus, golden-blond-haired and blue-eyed, as in the coloring books, full of relief.

When I wake, mist is heavy in the dawn trees. The male nurse is still there, but I don't care. At last I know what I need to do, what I have been guided to.

Lola paints my fingernails as red as Tara's toes. Lola paints my lips with sheer gloss. Lola hands me a white T-shirt and a skirt, and when Keats arrives, my hair is damp and freshly combed, I smell of shampoo.

'Hello, Betsy.'

'Hello, doctor.'

His skin is the color of milk.

'You look better today.'

I want to rise up and hold him, the way all the men held me, in the water in the bay.

I want to embrace him like Jesus, because he is so good to me.

'You had a rough night.'

He is half lit by the window, perfect in his shined shoes. 'You were angry,' he says.

Lola is smiling.

I am smiling, too.

'Betsy?'

He will think it is his fault. I feel bad about this. Sun breaks gold onto his smooth skin, his soft hands and wedding band.

'You are a good doctor.'

'Thank you.'

'You really are.'

'Are you saying goodbye?'

His hair, too, is damp from his morning shower. A curly brown lock hangs on his forehead.

'No,' I smile. 'That's your job.'

'Is it?'

'It's not your fault.'

What matters is that he remembers, when I am gone, that I was not angry with him.

'Something has changed.'

'Maybe.'

'You seem calm.'

'I feel calm.'

He sits on the desk chair, taking his time. Lola and I are on the bed.

'You smiled when I said we were moving you to Little House. As if you were pleased.'

'Why would I be pleased?'

'Maybe because I noticed.'

'Noticed what?'

'How bad you felt.'

'I guess you did.'

'And now you feel good.'

'I had a good dream.'

'Did you?'

'Yes, actually.' I laugh. 'Jesus was in it.'

'Really?'

'We went swimming.' I laugh again, so as not to alarm him. 'Actually, I'd quite like to go swimming now. Can I?'

'You're in Little House, Betsy.'

'So I can't swim?'

'You can't leave the house.'

'Not even with Lola?'

'Except for your sessions with me.'

'Do you really think that's necessary?'

'I do, yes.'

Little House is warm and dark, a square lounge in the center, small rectangular rooms off the slim corridor. They take my nail file, my mirror, my shoelaces and belt. Six of the ten beds are occupied and everyone is on House Restriction.

I see Keats every morning. I see him in the parking lot and at the doctors' office and on the steps to Little. I see him with the nurses, writing orders for my medication and meals. By now, he has seen me everywhere: in the lounge at Dobson House, in the swimming pool, at Treatment, and on the steps of the closed chapel. He has sat with me in his office, in nurses' stations, and in deck chairs. The only place he has not sat is on my bed.

'What has changed?' he asks.

'Something.'

'You're different.'

'Isn't that the idea?'

'The idea of what?'

'Fairley, Treatment, Little House.'

'I'd just like to know what affected you so much.'

'I don't know. I just feel like it's over.'

'What is?'

'The past. It's like I struggled with it for so long, and now it's over.'

'The past?'

'Yes.'

'Not your life?'

'Life as I've known it.'

Tess, the novelist's wife, is in Little for her hallucinations. She was on a day pass and saw the devil in a shop window.

'It was horrible,' she tells me, starting to weep.

'It sounds horrible.'

She nods. 'What you have to face,' she says—though what she says has nothing to do with me—'is that you are someone who can be left.'

* * *

Now that I have a plan, I feel assured. I feel light and beneficent and pure. I eat all my meals. I play Scrabble with Tess. I talk to Paula, who lifts her eyes to the trees.

David bashes against the walls, so they put him in restraints. They let the rest of us sit outside, on the strip of cement that is our sun deck. Jo passes by in jeans and a polo shirt and hiking boots.

'How are you?' I call out.

'Lonely.'

She wants to come see me. Keats won't allow it. Truth is, I am glad about this. I feel bad for her, her and her wide open eyes. I am afraid of her, too. She is an open door, a wind blowing through.

After five days, Keats takes me off Specials. 'Can I go to Rec. now?' I ask.

'Soon.'

The pool is the best place. Everything else is violent. Also, water is the best for me.

It was always water: in the harbor and the creek, the ocean and the pool. Once my mother saw us. She was coming down the hill, her dress long and blue.

'What are you doing?' she asked.

'Nothing,' Ray said. 'Run,' he said, so we did.

'I'd like us to talk about our relationship.'

'The one that's about to end?'

'You sound bitter.'

'I am not afraid.'

'I didn't say you were afraid.'

'Well, I'm not.'

'You had hopes about our relationship.'

'Is that bad?'

'When I said I couldn't see you, it was as if you had no worth.'

I pull my legs underneath me. 'I have worth.'

'You become deeply attached—to Frank, to Wayne, to Jo and me. Then when people leave, it's as if you don't exist.'

'That's not true.'

'What are you going to do next? After Fairley?'

'I don't want there to be an *After Fairley.*'

'Meaning?'

I laugh. 'You won't even talk to me after Fairley.'

'I can't talk to you after Fairley. There's no contact allowed for three years between patients and staff.'

'You never told me that.'

'You never gave me a chance.'

I feel better now, though I don't let on. 'It doesn't matter, anyway.'

'To me it does.'

I smile. 'I can't live my life for you.'

I feel sorry for him, a little, that he will get in trouble over me. Still, I can't help it.

'I feel like you're planning something.'

'You are very smart.'

'What is it?'

I want to tell him. I want him to be happy for me. I want to cry, also, because I am going to miss him.

'It's a good plan,' I say. 'You'd like it.'

'Don't you trust me?'

I do cry then. The water will be heavy and cool, dark and green. I have to bite my lip. 'No.'

He shakes his head, leaning close to me. 'I can't blame you.'

Even though I am quiet, happy as I have never been, Keats won't let me out. 'You're making a mistake,' I cry to him now.

'Am I?' he asks, and I think he knows, suddenly. I think he has guessed what I want.

He asks my parents to come in and I don't want them to. I am like a pond, I tell him. All these things just break the calm.

'They need to see you.'

'Why? So they can feel worse later?'

Truth is, too much time is passing. I want to walk into the pool, but at the same time, it is no longer seeming urgent. I like the idea of it as much as the action. I feel safe in the idea—as in a bed, resting. Also, I like Little House. I like my small room and the warm lounge and seeing Keats all day long, seeing him spend his time on me, his thought and energy on knowing everything, letting nothing go.

'Do you think your parents noticed what was going on between you and Raymond?'
     'Not really.'
     'But they knew how you felt about him?'
     'I would say so.'
     'They might have done something about that.'
     'They tried.'
     'How did they?'
     'They sent him away—to boarding schools, and then to Antigua.'
     'But he came back.'
     I nod.
     'How did that make you feel?'
     I stretch out my arms. 'Well—I'm not the center of the universe. I'm not the only one in the family.'
     'Is that what they told you?'
     I laugh. 'That is the sad truth.'

My parents are late. They are often late, actually. They get upset about it, but they're late anyway.
     'It must be boring,' I say to Keats as we wait, 'being a psychiatrist.'
     'How so?'
     'The way it all comes down to our parents. How they didn't give us enough attention or how they suffocated us. Or both.'
     'You're not going swimming.'
     'I'm not?'

'No.'

He has guessed. He has guessed but he doesn't say.

They arrive apologizing. When my mother hugs me, I see Keats over her shoulder, smiling at me. He is younger than my parents by about ten years, but my father doesn't argue with him. He is respectful—perhaps because he thinks Keats knows something he doesn't, from me.

There is only twenty minutes left for our session, though Keats says we can run over a little. He tells them about Little House, how there was an 'incident' between me and another patient.

'Was there a fight?' my father asks, smiling—as if he would expect such a thing from me.

Keats pauses.

'She did very well. She defended herself.'

'She's quite good at that, I think,' my father says.

'Actually, the reason I asked you up here is that we've been very worried about Betsy.'

My father's smile is his great defense. 'We're always worried about Betsy.'

'I think she has made a lot of progress.'

My father doesn't believe him. It makes me sick that he doesn't believe him.

'Eddie—' My mother touches his hand.

'It's all right,' Keats says. 'I was wondering if perhaps Raymond could come in for a session?' My parents look at each other. 'That seems like a good idea.'

'It is their problem, really, isn't it?' my mother says.

Afterwards, I am so upset, I cry into my hands in front of Keats. 'You must remember,' Keats says, 'what we are after.'

'Which is what?'

'Which is your care. Which is their agreeing to help pay for your care.'

When I lie back on my bed, when the sun is hot on my closed eyelids, I am almost there. Almost in the cool green where I want so much to be, the cool waters I have seen, the quiet and the flowing there.

I am quiet as air, I am filled with sun, and I am almost there.

Raymond calls Little House, and I take the telephone in the nurses' station, and Ray talks as if he has just seen me, as if everything is fine.

'What's going on?'

'You know.'

'Rehab,' he laughs. 'You were a little strung out.'

'I guess.'

'They want me to come up.'

'That's the thought.'

'As long as they don't try to get me to stay.'

'I don't think it's about that.'

'No?'

We are silent. I do not want to upset him. 'Well,' he finally says, 'whatever. I can do that.'

'All right then.'

'I'll see you soon.'

'Are you sure about this?' I ask Keats.

'I think you can handle it.'

I can't understand Ray putting himself in this position, putting himself before Dr. Keats and my parents and me.

'Maybe there's something in it for him,' Keats says, but I can't see it.

Henry stops by, unannounced, carrying his motorcycle helmet.

'Elizabeth.' He swings past the nurses' station. 'What are you doing?'

The nurses stop him, of course. No one is allowed in here without permission.

'What are *you* doing?' the head nurse asks him.

Henry isn't the way I am—he doesn't get angry or impatient at all. 'I'm sorry,' he says. 'My name is Henry Peake. I'm a friend of Betsy's.'

They are nice to him, but they don't let him inside. They send him up the hill to the doctors' office. He waves at me as he leaves, and comes back forty-five minutes later, a note from Keats in his hand.

'I thought this place was voluntary,' he says, as we sit on the cement porch in white plastic deck chairs.

'It is. But Little House isn't.'

He looks around. 'What did you do?' he asks, smiling.

'Not much. They're just—paranoid.'

He looks good: tan and relaxed, his hair longer than usual.

'Did you hear I was born again?'

'Something like that.'

'I would like to be born again,' he grins at me, 'with you.'

I laugh. 'Oh, please.'

He hands me a Marlboro.

'Were you baptized?'

'Three times: in Nevada, Texas, and Iowa City.'

'I thought you were writing your thesis this year.'

Henry shrugs. 'I was, but research is fun. Why graduate?'

His thesis is called 'The Effects of Ritual: Mass Hysteria or the Holy Spirit?'

'So what's the answer?' I ask.

'There isn't one.'

I smile. 'There isn't?'

'Well, it just depends who's looking at it.'

'And if you're the one looking?'

'I would side, at this point, with the Holy Spirit.'

'That's why you're born again.'

He laughs. 'Exactly.' Then he looks around at the grounds. 'Are they helping you here?'

'I like my doctor.'

'We could make a run for it, you know. On my bike.'

'My doctor wants me to go to Halfway House.'

'Oh yeah?'

'In Arizona.'

Henry squints, putting his cigarette butt in one of our sand buckets. 'Is this about your brother?'

'Somewhat.'

'You're talking to your doctor about him?'

'Oh, yes.'

He must be hot in his jeans, his jacket, black boots.

'Did you see that movie *Zabrinskie Point?*' I ask. 'Where everything is blown up at the end: houses, cars, bookshelves, cupboards?'

'Sure.'

'That was shot in Arizona.'

'I'll visit you.'

'Will you?'

'Of course. We can go to the Grand Canyon.'

He is so gentle, so good-looking and kind. I wish I could kiss him. Maybe he'd even like me to. I think this through and realize I am still fooling myself. I can't love him and probably never will.

Still, he is here.

PART VII

THE DREAM doesn't let go of me, so much as it spreads through me. It doesn't beckon me from the outside, but becomes part of me, 'in here,' as Beck used to say, all corny and serious, holding his fist to his chest.

Surprisingly, my parents are early. I am allowed to wait for them outside the doctors' office. I watch their silver Porsche pull up, my mother in sunglasses and Raymond stretched out in the backseat. Ray doesn't look so good. His face is bony and pale. He is high, I am sure, his hair dirty and his eyes stony blue. 'Hey,' he says, in his languid way.

'Hey.'

We all stand around at the top of the hill. My mother suggests Raymond and I go for a walk. I feel my parents watching us as we go. On the lawn, my boots slide on the damp grass. Raymond catches my arm. He looks tired. His black jacket is creased and smells of cigarettes. I feel clean beside him, my hair neatly combed, dress pressed. We stop near Dobson House, at the edge of the woods. Raymond has his back to our parents and lights a cigarette.

'So, how've you been?'

'All right.'

'I'm sorry about what happened.'

His eyes are nervous. He is slurring his words ever so slightly.

'When?'

'In Central Park—when the police came. I had to leave.'

He probably is sorry. That's the sad thing.

'I had all this coke on me. I just—I had to go.'

Dad is watching us from the hill, his hands in his leather jacket. My mother's jacket is leather also, not black, but ivory.

'Did you come back later?'

'Of course.'

'Really?'

'You were gone.'

I don't believe him. Still, he is trying.

Dad has pulled out his cellular phone and my mother is redoing her ponytail.

'You like being sober?'

'I feel all right.'

'Do you?'

'Sometimes.'

'That's pretty good.'

The sun is bright but not warm.

'This place looks nice.'

He flicks his cigarette to the ground. He misses the cigarette bucket. 'I'll tell them . . . whatever you want, you know. I won't deny it.' I nod. 'Then I'm going to Montana again.' I stare at him, skinny as a teenager and sicklier.

'Montana?'

'Why not?'

My father waves from the hill. 'You could stop, too,' I say.

'No.'

Why should it mean anything for Ray to speak? Why should the future change like a landscape beneath weather? How could my life be split in two?

We all meet Keats in the waiting room, on the peach couch by the Chippendale chairs. Keats takes Raymond back to his office. 'I am going outside,' I say, not feeling so well suddenly.

'I'll walk with you,' my mother says.

I haven't been alone with her in a long time. I am not sure I want to be. We stand at the top of the hill, an autumn wind blowing.

'You must be nervous,' my mother says, looking out over the lawn, the lawn I ran down, before they put me in Little House.

'I guess I am.'

She is wearing the cornflower blue earrings I mailed to her.

'I wanted to tell you something.'

I don't want her to tell me anything.

'Wayne has moved to Belgium, permanently.'

'He has?'

'Last month.'

'You saw him?'

'He phoned.'

'He did?' My mouth starts to tremble.

'I wish you had told me,' my mother says.

'Told you what?'

'It's been a shock for all of us.'

I nod.

'I can't be a hypocrite. I can't say I don't understand.' She levels her blue eyes on me. 'I do think he shouldn't have done what he did.'

She takes my hand. Her skin is so soft.

'But he already has a family, Betsy.'

In Keats's office, Raymond has the window open, smoking a cigarette. The shrubs outside smell like pepper and I am afraid something terrible is going to happen—some disaster or interruption so Raymond will have to leave. It doesn't, though, and when it doesn't, I feel for sure when he has finished talking that my life has snapped in half, a branch in the hand.

*

Arizona will be hot and dry. I will live with people my age and get a job making cappuccinos or some such thing.

My bags are packed when Eric arrives in his car. I have permission to run up to the doctors' office, at seven-fifty a.m., to say goodbye.

Keats smiles as I come into his room.

'Ready?' he asks.

'What do you think?'

'I don't know.'

'Do you think I'll make it?'

'I hope so.'

'A soul that has been fractured can be entered.'

'Very nice.'

'Kung Fu. It was on television, last night.'

He laughs. He steps to me and kisses me on the cheek, holding on to my shoulders.

I miss him already.

I miss him so I put him inside, where my dream is, the constant water in light.

Then I run, out the door and down to the car where Eric is waiting, and suddenly we are gone.

Also from AKASHIC BOOKS

SPEAK NOW by Kaylie Jones
A new novel from the author of A SOLDIER'S DAUGHTER NEVER CRIES
247 pages, hardcover, $22.95, ISBN: 1-888451-53-X

"*Speak Now* is one of those rare novels that fuses the craft of the narrative with the art of characterization: a page-turner cast with complex characters including the addicted, the haunted, and the doers of good deeds. Ms. Jones is to be commended, too, for her vivid portrayals of the experiences and memories of Holocaust victims, who contribute touching and ironic commentary to this tale of contemporary lives of frequently self-inflicted pain."
—Sidney Offit, author of *Memoir of the Bookie's Son*

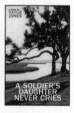

A SOLDIER'S DAUGHTER NEVER CRIES by Kaylie Jones
200 pages, trade paperback, $13.95, ISBN: 1-888451-46-7

The inspiration for the Merchant Ivory film starring Kris Kristofferson, Barbara Hershey, and Leelee Sobieski, *A Soldier's Daughter Never Cries* is a rich and poignant family story from the daughter of novelist James Jones (*From Here to Eternity, The Thin Red Line*). This brand new edition includes an author's introduction and a new chapter; "Mother's Day."

"Every page is a joy." —*Self Magazine*

THE ICE-CREAM HEADACHE by James Jones
235 pages, trade paperback, $13.95, ISBN: 1-888451-35-1

Jones's only collection of stories back in print, with a new preface by daughter Kaylie Jones; and a brand new study guide.

"The thirteen stories are anything but dated . . . a compact social history of what it was like for Mr. Jones's generation to grow up, go to war, marry, and generally, to become people in America." —*The Nation*